TISHA

SINMISOLA OGÚNYINKA

The story is purely fictional and represents the craft and imagination of the author.

Any coincidence of the fictional names and places with real persons, living or dead, and real places, is unintentional.

Cover Design by Baseline Creatives © 2015

Image of man on the cover courtesy of Photo stock at FreeDigitalPhotos.net © 2015

Author Photo by Cybermul © 2010

CONTENTS

TISHA is dedicated to my mother, Agnes Tinuola Ifaturoti, a great teacher, mother and friend.

TISHA

CHAPTER 1

PUNISHMENT

My heart thuds at the mere prospect.

I will have to do something or lose total respect. I look at the three girls in front of me. The class is dead silent.

I train my eyes on Bisi, the smartest of the three. "Why did you cheat?"

"Ah, Tisha please. Me no shit!"

It's amazing how a girl so smart and pretty could have such a depressing diction.

"It's cheat. Ch ch."

"Sh sh."

"Anyway, that is not my issue now. I saw you sharing your paper with these other two and I am not going to take it lightly." I look at the other girl, Foyeke. "What happened, you?"

Foyeke rolls her eyes and shrugs. I've been told she's the daughter of the local chief and that's more than a piece of information.

I turn to Alape, the dumbest of them all. "Why did you copy from Bisi?"

Alape can't speak a word in English. "I did not," she says in the local dialect.

I hold my breath to keep from giving her a slap on the face. I could barely speak their language though I understood a little.

"You're lying. Bisi, tell me the truth."

She was just so pretty. Her hair always plaited in thick rows show clean fair coloured lines separating whichever design it was. Today, Bisi's hair has been plaited in a style, which leaves the long dark ends falling over her face. I notice she likes to sweep them away when she talks.

I should not be attracted to her.

Bisi sobs. "No, sir. It just is is Alape is—"

"Shut up your dirty mouth!" Foyeke says in vernacular. She rolls into a long string of reprimand I could pick just a few words like 'snitch' from.

"I am going to punish all of you. I will give you zero."

"Ah, sero! Sero in Englis. Ah Tisha, please."

I can't bear to see her crying. I wave them to their seats. The class erupts in a chatter and I have to bring them under control.

"Quiet!"

This can't be where I should be. I develop a headache. Each time these local children make noise or annoy me, I get a headache. I've been with them for one month and I hate every day of it. After the first week, I applied for transfer from here but it's still under process.

"If you don't shut up, you will see my wrath."

There's some quiet but I can hear Foyeke's distinct thick voice with her accent so annoying, I could shut her up forever. I ignore and draw in deeper breathes. I should be out of their class in another few minutes and then I can gain my composure.

I walk to the teacher's desk in the class and arrange the exam sheets I just collected from the students. Why am I so angry?

These children cheat in the exams and tests all the time.

"Tisha, please. No give me sero."

I look up. Bisi stands in front of the desk, her face wet. "Teacher please, don't give me zero."

She shakes her head, the soft curly locks swirl around. I look away and catch Foyeke stare at us from her seat in the middle of the class.

She's full of disdain, and I raise my voice. "Then I will give you twelve strokes each."

The village children are not new to being flogged. The school principal makes it a daily ritual.

"These children are so stubborn and evil, until you whip the devil out of them, they cannot learn," the principal says all the time.

I must be out of my mind to say this. Flog the girls? Flog Bisi? Why did I say that? I look at the object of my confused emotions, and she nods.

"Thank you, sir."

She loved reading and studying. I don't want to punish her. I don't want to hurt her. She's thanking me for my choice to hurt her. Dear Lord, what have I said?

The class captain, a tough eighteen-year-old boy I chose because he was the oldest and toughest, brings a cane within a minute.

I have never hit anyone in my life. Without any invitation, Foyeke and Alape come to stand in front of the class.

The other teachers whip these kids all the time. Now I have allowed my anger to put me in a fix.

Foyeke is arrogant about it. She steps forward and stretches her hand before me. My anger is justified. These are girls in their penultimate year in high school. I should treat them like ladies.

I hit on her hand. This is right. The other teachers beat these stubborn kids.

When the last stroke lands on Foyeke's hand, she licks her lips and looks at me. In her thickest accent ever, she speaks vernacular. "You will hear from my father."

The class erupts in laughter. She walks to her seat amidst an applause.

I ignore. Alape steps forward and within minutes, I've discharged justice.

Bisi has tears in her eyes, and my heart drops into my stomach. There's a cheer and I turn to see Alape giving high fives to her seat mates.

I raise the cane, and Bisi closes her eyes the same time she stretches her hand out. I have to do it, and I do.

Bisi lets out a blood-curling scream. The class roar in laughter.

The cane drops from my hand and clatters on the dirt floor.

CHAPTER 2

APOLOGY

I **shake uncontrollably.**

Bisi grabs her assaulted hand with the other and doubles over. My heart heaves. I'm sorry, I couldn't say it though. I bend and pick the cane. She straightens as well, and slowly stretch out the assaulted hand again.

"Go to your seat," I blurt. I clench my teeth to keep from shaking and throw the cane aside.

I can't stop shaking. I can't get the sound of her scream out of my head. I can't get the sight of her blistered hand out of my mind. She's so fair-skinned. The fairest in the class.

God, help me not to notice these things.

The class raises a cheer. I'm beyond care. I pack my books and leave the class though I still had at least ten minutes of the period.

I rush to the staff room, and thankfully, none of the teachers are present. It's still morning; just the second period. I need to get my poise before I can attend the other classes I have.

I place my head on my table and draw air into my lungs. Involuntarily, I loosen my tie. A few minutes and I know I'll be fine. It becomes more apparent that I need to leave Abagboro village. Before I commit the unthinkable. Having a crush on a village girl? That's about the most absurd thing on earth.

Back in Lagos, one of the training I have is to dare not get emotionally attached to a student. I had chosen post-primary education as my major because I have a passion to see these teenagers off the streets and on the path of destiny.

My last posting to Community Girls High in Lagos hadn't presented a least challenge. Why here in this hell-hole where all the villagers smell the same. Except Bisi. She must have a bath in the village stream daily.

I leap to my feet and pace. You can't think like that, Abbey. Sophisticated Lagos girls did not meet your fancy, why should this girl do?

I just need to get out of here. I am still appalled at being posted here. This is not a good sign. This is the more reason why I should not be here.

The bell goes off to signify the end of one period and the beginning of another. I teach all the senior classes and there's hardly a free period for me during the week.

With a resolve I cannot summon, I walk to my table and arrange my workbook. I have a final year class next. Because of the level of understanding of these students, I've had to devise a system of giving them several exams before the main one, which could be used to substitute part of their marks in the final exam.

The principal thought I was too lenient but I made him understand a good SSCE (Senior Secondary Certificate Examination) result in English from his school will improve his profile, and he agreed.

"Tisha, sorry."

I look up and Bisi is on her knees. I had not heard her walk in.

My heart flops to the base of my feet. I frown. "Stand up."

She erupts in a flow of vernacular about what happened.

"Haven't I told you, you must never speak Yoruba to me?"

"Sorry, sir."

"Stand up. Don't you have a class now?"

"Is free period sir. For me."

"Well, I have a class." I brush past her and escape.

Toro, my co-student teacher, though from another college and city, meet me at the entrance. Her face is beclouded. The poor girl has had things tougher than me here. The first week of our arrival, she had reacted violently to the water, breaking out in pus-filled blisters.

"Toro?"

"I just got a letter. Government has a new policy for student teachers. Effective immediately."

I need to leave this place before I mess myself up. I don't need any gloomy policies. I shrug. Toro hands me a letter. It's from my department. I tear the letter open, and read.

It's all bad.

"It's the same thing, right?"

I heave. "It's a rejection of my transfer from here."

Toro sighs. "Well, that means it's the same. The new policy is strict on transfers. And posting for final year students is no longer three but six months."

My mouth drops open.

Toro clamps her lips. "We're here for the next five months, Abbey. I want to die."

Bisi walks by us and down the corridor to her class. I didn't know my gaze followed her.

CHAPTER 3

TORO

I'm in the middle of reading and dozing when Toro knocks on my door and enters.

I fold the page on my John Grisham novel and sit up. Most evenings I read, and I like to be alone but she's my neighbour, and she's been a lot of help to me, I must confess. She cooks and shares with me.

The principal of Abagboro Community High School gives accommodation to student teachers on the school premises, which is great. It's quiet and lonely after school hours but I like it. The accommodation is not much but far better than what we'd have gotten if we rent in the village.

Here at least there's a little kitchenette for cooking, though all rooms share a bathroom and toilet at the end of the corridor. The bathroom, separate from the toilet, has a shower and toilet space has a shank. Both share a little space where the wash hand basin is placed. My kitchenette is dry and dusty. I am still grateful. It's better than what I had in Lagos, in some way. A government grant had been used to build the accommodation, which is about the most modern building in the village.

Two blocks were built and some teachers live in one block. Our block has four rooms but only mine and Toro's are currently occupied.

Toro sits on the edge of my bed pushed against the wall in the small room. She tries to be friendly but I've never had close girlfriends. She smiles and takes the John Grisham from me.

"What are you reading?"

I shrug. "A time to kill."

She gasps and draws herself closer. "I watched the movie. The black man who killed two white boys for raping—"

"Hey don't tell me, I just started it."

She laughs. "Sorry. It's a good read. You'll like it."

I smile. "I like it already."

"I could do with a good book right now. It's so boring in this village. I hate it." She stretches and relaxes against my wall, which looked so awkward because now she is more in the bed than me.

I stand. I'm not all that comfortable around women. At twenty-one, I've had a lot of opportunities to get women's attention but I'm not interested. I'm more into my work, and my family. Raised by a single mother, my sister and I have always had it drilled into our heads to focus on education and career, first.

I walk to my single wardrobe and open it. "I have another Grisham here. The Chamber."

"I've read it."

I squat in front of my rucksack full of novels. "Let me see. Do you read Baldacci?"

"No."

I hear the groan of my spring bed, and sense she has moved only a second before she crouches behind me. I feel her at once. All of her softness engulf me. If I straighten, I'll push her away and I don't like the sound of that.

"No, you don't or no you haven't."

Her hand rests on my hip. "No, I haven't. What's it like?"

Her pointed chin rests on my shoulder. "Like Grisham I guess. Here." I need to stand. Without being cheeky, she adds pressure on my back. I have to get Toro out of my room. She's a beautiful woman. Fair-skinned as well, and slender, curvy. She wears her hair in a stylish funk around her oblong face. Her best attributes are her bosom. Much as I hate to admit it to myself.

She presses that amazing part of her anatomy on my back. I ease up, taking her with me.

"Here, you'll like this one."

"First Family. Hmm." She moves away, taking her musky scent with her. "What's it about?"

I choose not to join her on my bed. I lean against the wardrobe. "Read it. Hey, if I tell you why would you want to read?"

She laughs. "Makes sense." She sighs. "Have you had any dinner?"

"Left over from yesterday. Then I marked the scripts for my students' exams."

"That yellow girl who came to the staff room with you." She purses her full lips. "What did she want?"

I shrug. "She—" Suddenly I'm unable to say what I did. More for Bisi's sake. I don't want Toro to see her as a cheat. "Nothing really. Can I remember? These girls come to ask all sorts of funny questions all the time."

"Hmm. Just be careful. I hate these village girls. They are so rotten. You'll be shocked."

I can still feel Toro's imprint on my back. So who's rotten? "I don't bother myself with them."

"Just be careful. Especially that one. And that village head's daughter. You'll be shocked what I hear about them."

I didn't want to know. "I will be." I scratch my head. "So what did you have for dinner?"

"I've not eaten. Thought we'll eat together."

"Ah, sorry."

"Well, I'm hungry." She stands. "I may come back with my food if this novel doesn't hook me."

I smile. "Fine. I'm not getting to sleep for another two hours or so."

She checks her mobile phone. "Ah, two hours. This is almost eight. I should be asleep if the book—"

"Doesn't hook you. It will."

She waves and leaves. I heave a heavy sigh. Toro's been giving off all these signals since the first day we met a month ago but pressing herself on me like that? A bad sign.

I'd better get my act together and let her know her place.

CHAPTER 4

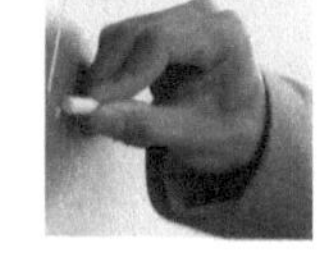

WATER TROUBLE

I **wake to disturbance outside.**

On impulse, I reach for my phone and check the time. 4a.m. What the heck? I reach for my trousers tossed over the back of my chair and get dressed. For a moment, I stand to listen again. I listen for Toro but hear nothing distinct. Voices, footfalls, and water rushing.

I pick my phone instead of barging out to the unknown in this ridiculous village where they talk funny, and call Toro.

She picks on the fifth ring. "Yes?"

I must admit she sounds different from sleep. "Are you okay? Do you hear sounds outside?"

"Yes. They're villagers. Fetching water from our tap."

I pull my curtain aside. Fear has torment indeed. "There's no water in the village?"

"Looks like it, Abbey. Please I want to sleep."

She cut the line. Hmm. I stare at the rush outside. Toro and I share a bathroom, and toilet, but a tap has been fixed just outside her window. If there's no water in the village, then there may soon be a shortage here as well.

How did these villagers know we'd have water here? In my one month of being in Abagboro village, there has been water. I never imagined it would be a problem. I didn't have a bucket to store water or …

I hear a sharp sound outside, and behold. Two men are in a fight. One hit the other with his metal bucket. Blood spurts forth. I grip the curtain. I cannot involve myself, and the villagers arrive in troves. The two men are ignored as more people crowd around the tap.

I drop the curtain and get back in bed. Of course, I can't sleep. I prepare for the day instead. I go into our bathroom where there's only one bucket Toro bought. I take a bath and fill the bucket with water.

To while the time, I dig into my John Grisham. It's too early to be awake but what can I do? I must have dozed after a while because I startle awake at 7a.m. All is quiet.

I listen for any movements, none. I hear Toro hum in the next room. Good, all must be well then. I'm not a breakfast person, so I take a cup of tea in my normal manner.

Assembly is at eight and I don't have to be there though I make it a duty. The walk from our accommodation to the school area is five minutes. I have time on my hands.

There's a knock, and Toro enters. Sometimes I wonder if she hopes to catch me naked the way knocks and enters without invitation.

"The tap is spoilt." She sighs. "We are going to have water troubles."

"Good morning. What tap? The one outside?"

"Yes. Two men nearly killed themselves over that tap and with the rush and all, the tap was twisted and couldn't be shut. Water's been rushing out without control." She sighs again. "Anyway, I filled our bucket. We need something to store the water because I don't know what will happen."

"Where's the source of the water?"

She shrugs. "I don't know. I'm going to school."

With that, she exits. So temperamental.

I walk round the back of our rooms to assess the damage. The whole area is swamped and the tap is still on. There's a black nylon around the mouth of the tap, a good person's effort to staunch the flow. Not effective though. I go back inside my room and get another nylon bag and succeed only in getting myself wet.

I wonder what the source is. How life forces one to make enquiries.

The principal gets to inspect the tap three days later. Maybe it was a mistake to invite him. The water is sourced from a bore-hole, which the school pumps water for the whole compound.

After the principal visited, he stopped pumping the water pending the time the tap is fixed. There began the water trouble. The village source from government-operated water works had ceased. Now, there's nowhere to get water except the stream.

Toro had bought a keg and a small drum and stored water before the shutdown. Thank God for women. I never envisaged any problem.

But after a week, and the tap had still not been fixed, and our little drum and keg of water were diminished, I decide to call a plumber and do it myself.

CHAPTER 5

SUMMARY

The stench in the class is worse.

With no water in the village, the stream has turned from being the rejected stone to the cornerstone. My ordeal with the stream is better left untold.

I pop two mint sweets into my mouth and turn to the chalk board. I haven't made much progress with this class, and they are less than five months away from the mock exam. I'm not able to use the right textbook because most of them know nothing. I resorted to the textbook being used two classes lower.

"Summary. Open your book to page 50 in your English textbook. Look at the passage there." I write summary on the board and turn. I drop the chalk close to my teacher's workbook and look at them. "Who can read for us?" I look around. "Yes?"

The students look at one another.

"You are writing your exam in about four months and you can't read a simple passage?"

A hand goes up. The only one that usually did. "Segi, yes?"

The girl stands. "Today, Si-ne-se—"

I look at my book. "Chinese."

"Saineese. Today, Saineese food is weh know around de word, and re...re...re—"

"Recipes."

"Re-si-pis for Saineese cook can be *fond* in most cook-book and on—"

I scratch my head. "Do you understand what you are reading?" I sigh.

A part of me wants to read it all but they need to learn to read. Most of them would end up on the streets of the village anyway. They will become farmers and traders like their parents. There's a slim chance, one, maybe only one will move on to college. For the sake of that one, I take a deep breath and look at Segi.

"Continue."

"Re-si-pis for Saineese cook can be *fond* in most cook-book and on many wabe-seet. Wabe-seets. While book wit some in-for-ma-son about ah-n-ci-cin-cint Saineese food haf sor-fi-fe de cen-cen-tu-ri fask-cin-cinna-ting new informason ha come moh reck-cenli from tom-bi."

She looks at me. And I stare back sure she must have a headache coming like me.

"Thank you. You may have your seat. I will read it again and please listen carefully." I pause for effect. "Today, Chinese food is well known around the world, and recipes for Chinese cooking can be found in most cookbooks and on many web sites." I look to see if I had their attention. I did. "While books with some information about ancient Chinese food have survived the centuries, fascinating new information has come more recently from tombs."

I read it two more times. Then I tell them to answer the questions after the short paragraph. While they do, I contemplate the next paragraph they have to read. How harder could it get.

For the next thirty minutes, I pop mint sweet and endure the reading. I have to do it. The former teacher who taught English had cared less. I'd been told the last set of graduates scored 100% failure in English.

I can't save them all. But maybe one or two will pull through.

"You will go home and read the passage from the beginning to the end. Tomorrow, we are having a test."

The class goes up in protest.

"Quiet."

"Ah Tisha, efry day tes tes tes."

"Yes, you will have tests every day till I am satisfied you know what you're doing." I smile. "We were supposed to start on summary today but you can't even read the passage."

I pack my books and walk out amidst boos. They can't be blamed. Previous teachers taught them English in vernacular.

CHAPTER 6

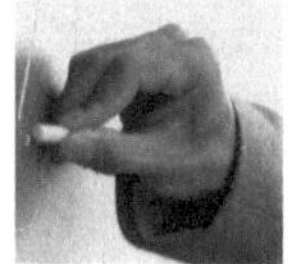

THE REJECTED STONE

Each evening for days now, I have to fetch water from the stream, after the villagers have gone.

Toro and I discovered a part further upstream where the water is clean and so we fetch from there.

The plumber I found lived in Ife, a big town east of Abagboro and about two hours trek away. He'd examined our tap and promised to return with materials to fix it. That was four days earlier.

I bend my bucket over the water. Toro had pleaded that I fetch for her as well, lazy bones. She stretches her luck with me sometimes, which is so annoying. I'm careful to take the clear water for the keg first.

The stream is narrow around here and trees from the small bush hang down, which makes the area cooler, and remote.

Since the water trouble started, I've learned to balance the 50-litre keg on my head, and hold two buckets on days Toro refuses to join me. It's the only option to making two trips.

I hum a popular song by Ice Prince and do not notice the swift movements before I see them.

Three village boys stand in a semi-circle, and stare at me. I drop my bucket and give them my full attention. They're dressed in the local manner with the village boys, unmatched print trousers with dirty shirts of different colours. They can't be more than sixteen years old each, but with these poverty-stricken villagers, they could be family men.

"Tisha! You think you have power in this village because you can speak English." The statement in heavily-accented vernacular is from a stout dark-skinned one. "You think because you wear tie around your neck like a goat, you can harass our girls."

I frown. I speak a little Yoruba, and I respond with it. "I never harass any girls."

I didn't see it coming, or I could have dodged at least. Another one, not much taller than the first speaker, flips a cow-whip in a flash. It catches me across my face to my chest. I gasp, the shock and pain mixed in equal proportion. I straighten, and decide to leave rather than fight. I've never been a fighting person, and would rather resort to dialogue, but these ruffians didn't look like they wanted to talk. The keg is almost full and I can come back for more water. I pick it along with my two empty buckets.

"Where do you think you're going?" The whipping boy says.

I heave. "I don't want any trouble."

The first talker stand in front of me. "Then why did you look for it?"

The whipping boy lifts his whip again and this time I step aside, but he doesn't hit me. The third quiet one moves close and tackles me. I fight back but he is mighty strong. Soon I understand their plan. The third one and the speaker hold my head, arms and legs and for the life of me, prostrated on the floor, I knew.

The whip says, "How many did you say?"

"Twelve," the speaker says.

The whip is painful. Faced down on the wet bank of upstream, two village boys strapping me in a death grip, the three boys count as the whip unleashes twelve strokes on my behind. *"Eni, eji, eta, erin—"*

I doubt if I will be able to sit for days.

"There," the speaker says. "Learn your lessons, Tisha, and don't look for trouble from the princess next time."

Within seconds, they are gone. I remain as they left me, face down on the wet banks, the pain coursing through my body, and I weep like a little child.

CHAPTER 7

PEACE

Despite my many protests, Toro insists on tending to my backside.

"You have to make a report, Abbey," she says over and over again. "What is the meaning of this? In fact, you have to make a report."

She brings out her smartphone and takes pictures of me.

"I report and they get in trouble, and the next time, I die in my sleep. Thanks but no thanks," I say.

She wears me down about treating me anyway. I lie on my stomach, and she cleans my butt with liquid antiseptic. I bite my pillow to keep from crying. It takes me a minute before I realize she's taking pictures of that side as well.

Unfortunately for me, I can't jump up much as I wish. "What on earth are you doing?"

"This is evidence, Abbey. If you don't plan to use it, I do."

I moan. "Use it for what?"

"To apply for a transfer from this hell-dump."

"Of course not." I jerk up and wince. "You won't use pictures of my butt to apply for your transfer."

"And yours as well." She chuckles. "If this picture reaches my head of department, they'll give me less than 24 hours to get out of here."

She takes a few more shots from different angles and then covers me with a wrapper. I hate her at that moment but she's right. If there's any report of assault, I will be transferred to another school. Which is such a good idea. But the humiliation of having to recant my ordeal is overwhelming.

"Please, Toro. Don't do this to me. Don't show pictures of my—"

She winks. "Trust me, Abbey. I'll be discreet. You'll need to make a report to your school as well."

"Or else yours will have no basis." I smile despite my pains. "Thanks for pointing it out."

"You wish. Whether you report or not, I'm filing for transfer based on this assault, no water and lack of concern by the school authorities."

"You'll be implicating many people." I snicker. "I pray for you, Toro. That the boys who assaulted me will not feel offended and come on to you."

"I'm a big girl. I can take care of myself." She closes the door behind her, and then shouts. "We still need to get water since you came back with none."

Tough luck.

The following morning, I force myself to get to school. The students would expect me not to be there. The pain on my behind has settled in and spread through my body. I have to walk like my body is in a cast but I refuse to look at any of the students in Bisi's class.

Many thoughts cross my mind on what to do for revenge but as they come, I push them out. If I react, then they have won. My only concern is Toro. I need to stop her from making any reports.

Foyeke makes several implicating and provocative statements throughout the class period but I ignore. I may not be a village boy but I'm metal. I don't dissolve in fire. Bisi giggles a few times. I think of asking them to stand in front of the class and read, or give the whole class a test, but each thought is swallowed up by the peace I feel within me.

I may not win with my cane, but these village kids will break under my will. I am resolved on this.

CHAPTER 8

ARRIVALS

Mr. Akande, principal of Abagboro Community High School calls for a meeting in the staff room and cancels all the classes remaining for the day.

It's Friday so the students close an hour earlier. I have only one period left, and glad I can return to my room and rest. The painkillers I took have worn off and I feel a fever coming.

The staff room fills up, and Mr. Akande walks in with three young men clad in the national youth service uniforms. A lady joins in later.

My heart jumps into my throat. We have youth corpers! I pray one can teach English and I can have some rest.

Mr. Akande steps forward. "Are we not lucky in this town? The National Youth Service Corps sent us four. Four. Four new arrivals. Abagboro Community, you are blessed."

Did he just say, town? How could a learned man be so deceived? Mr. Akande is in his sixties, and looks like the typical principal of a local school. His fashion is old and dated and he does nothing to tend to his shaggy hair or potbelly.

"The first is—" Akande looks into the sheet of paper in his hand. "Fortuna Osu—Usunna."

"Osondu, sir." The lady amongst the four step forward. "Fortuna Osondu."

"Miss Fortuna Osondu will teach biology for senior classes and integrated science for junior classes."

Akande smiles at her. She steps back. I'm amazed Mr. Akande doesn't use glasses considering the number of times he squints and blinks.

The current biology teacher Mr. Ojo, a tall, thin man in his forties, clap. Alone.

"Mr. Steve Eko."

Steve Eko steps forward. He is tall and well built, and good-looking. A small sound escapes from somewhere beside me, and I look at Toro. Her jaw is slack and there's this lost look in her eyes.

"Eko? Does your name mean Lagos?"

Steve arches his eyebrow. "No, principal."

Not a very friendly guy, I think. At least he could have taken a joke.

"Mr. Steve Eko will teach biology."

Mr. Ojo clap louder and laughs.

Toro frowns. "Ah, biology again. What about math?"

Mr. Akande beams. "We have math teacher. Mr. Kenny Taiwo."

Kenny Taiwo is short and thickly set. He steps forward. "Good afternoon teachers. I'm glad to be here."

A few teachers mumble a response. I look round the room. Altogether with the new arrivals, we're less than twenty. Imagine the pressure the teachers in this school have had. How did any education department in the state expect these teachers to achieve any form of success?

"Last but not least, Mr. Christian Jang. He will teach physics and chemistry."

No English. I'm so depressed I don't know what to do with myself.

Mr. Akande clasps his hands. "So let us welcome all the new teachers and help them to enjoy this service year. I hope you will apply to stay with us after your one year of service."

Toro snickers and I chuckle. Mr. Akande is about the most deceived man on earth.

"We will make their tables and chairs available in the staff room in another week. Meanwhile, please share your space with them." He looks round. "They will join Mr. Abbey Ilori and Miss Toro Adelu at the quarters the school provided for accommodation."

I speak without thought. "There's no water there, sir. How will we all cope?"

"The plumber is working on it now as I speak." Akande claps. "So let's welcome them, introduce ourselves and what we teach."

"Thank God," I mutter.

I can't feel any gratitude toward Akande. He's old and sloppy and this environment can only dictate why.

We all do the introductions. I watch the young men and woman with pity in my soul. One year in this rotten village didn't seem like a pleasurable thing to wish anyone.

"Huh, Mr. Abbey, let me see you in my office." Mr. Akande beckons. "Miss Toro, please show the new arrivals to the accommodation." He turns and leaves.

The teachers throng round the youth corpers. I remember when I first arrived too. Then Toro was given more attention though because she's a babe to look at.

I walk over to the corpers and shake them each. I notice the short stocky math corper seem to coo over Toro while the hunk named "Lagos" stand too close for comfort.

"You'll please excuse me. I'll join you later after I see the principal. Welcome again."

I doubt they heard me. Toro is engaging them all, even the Fortuna. I walk to the end of the corridor and knock on Mr. Akande's door.

"Come in."

I take a deep breath and open the door. I have no idea what he wants.

"Principal."

"Yes. I would have asked you to sit but you may not be able to do so."

He presses his lips together. I dread what he wants to discuss. Toro! I could kill her.

"Open your *yansh*, Mr. Abbey. I want to see it."

CHAPTER 9

YANSH WAR

Mr. Akande is insufferable.

Could have been better if he had anything to offer. I am beside myself with anger and humiliation as the old man inspects the *yansh*. I plan all the words I will give Toro. It's just been three days since the flogging. I've not let her see it since that first day but she's been busy with her plan, obviously.

"Aha? Na rod they use beat you?"

I begin to pull up my trousers. He yelps. "No, let me look. Aha. These useless village boys. I told you they are demons in human form."

I roll my eyes. I'd tried to catch a glimpse of the damage done to me but could see a part only. It looks bad. Deep welts cut across my butt and part of my lower back and upper thigh. I've been forced to clean it by myself with antiseptics every day, and self-prescribed antibiotics.

"Did you see their faces?"

"Yes, but I can't recognize them if I see them now."

Mr. Akande looks at me. "You have to recognize them o. Your colleague wrote to state department and copied federal. With pictures!

The commissioner called perm sec, who called DG who called my boss, who called me. Showing me pictures of your—your yansh."

I pull up my trousers. "Well, maybe if there is a line-up at the village square, I may know them. For now—"

Mr. Akande frowned. "Let me see it again."

"It's healing now. I don't feel so much pain. I'm taking antibiotics." I clench my teeth. "Can I go now, sir?"

He raises his eyebrows. "You don't want to make a big deal about this, I see." He smiles and exposes a surprising set of even, white teeth. Interesting I never saw him smile before.

He pats my back. "Smart boy."

I walk my 'cast' walk out of his office, fuming. Toro has to pay for this. Well, she'll definitely have to prove to the state department my butt is not photoshopped. I wonder how she got to send the pictures. She must have travelled to Ife to do that because there's no business centre here.

I've totally forgotten about the new arrivals, consumed by my plans to retaliate, until I approach our accommodation.

I hadn't been gone that long and they are still packing their stuff into the rooms. Since there are three guys and a girl, and only two rooms, I suppose the girl will take a room and the three boys will share a room. How that sounds a little selfish to me. I begin to realize I may have a roommate from tonight. Awful.

They are all graduates, older. The youngest of them look at least three years older than me. The Chris Jang or what was his name. The stocky math teacher look at least eight years older. Maybe more. I swallow and advise myself quickly. I will not argue if they ask to share.

Fortuna notices me first. "Hi, Abbey right?"

I nod. "Yes. Welcome again."

"Ah we've been waiting for you. The guys want to see your room so we'll know how to share."

"Oh of course." I rush to my door.

"Though the other girl, what's her name?"

"Toro."

"Yeah, she says your room is the smallest."

"I never knew that."

"So I'm thinking I should take your room, and you can move to a bigger room with one of the guys."

I open my door wide, and go to inspect the other rooms. There's one big one, double mine, and the other is the same as mine. The Jang guy and short stocky are in the room. Toro and Mr. Lagos are nowhere in sight.

"Hello."

The two turn.

"Ah, you're here," Jang says.

"Sorry what are your names again? I'm Abbey."

"Kenny Taiwo. I teach math." He sticks out his thick hand to me and I shake him.

"I'm Christian Jang from Jos."

I'm impressed. "You've come a long way."

"Thank you."

Kenny claps. "So how do we share this space? I think Fortuna should take this one. Three of us can share the bigger one."

I shrug. "I can share my space with one person." It's only polite to offer. I remember they are my seniors. I'm just a student teacher. And when I'm gone in five months' they'll still be here.

"That's so nice of you, Abbey," Kenny says.

"I'll move in with Abbey," Jang says.

"That's settled then. So Fortuna can take this room and Steve and I will use the bigger space."

Fine by me. Where is the nonsense Toro? I wish I could attack her in front of these strangers. Humiliate her. Say a few nasty things about her so they know the kind of silly person she is.

But I know I cannot. The yansh war will have to wait till we're alone.

CHAPTER 10

MR. LAGOS

I **don't see Toro till the end of the day.**

She has vanished with Steve Eko aka Mr. Lagos. The others speculate they may have gone to 'town' together. I assist Jang in settling down in my room. The space is small, the bed as well, but we're men so no problems there.

I'm thankful the water is back or how would we have coped. Six adults sharing a bathroom and toilet. No water. That would have been a disaster. As it is with Toro and me, we bicker over who washes the toilet. I get that work most of the time because she shares her food with me.

Jang pushes his shoes under the bed. "So how do you eat here?"

"Toro cooks."

He chuckles. "You give her money to cook for you?"

"No. Ah." I laugh. "She shares her food."

"She must be very generous."

I shrug. And annoying. "She is. But most times I just buy bread from the village and take tea."

"Typical bachelor." Jang looks around. "I like to eat real food so if I can't cook, I must find where they sell."

"Well, food was important to me till I got here. Their food is different."

"I expected that. On camp I had to eat 'amala' that ugly black thing. The guys used to go to mami market and buy food. But that gets costly."

"I'm not much of a food person."

Jang looks me over. "It shows."

"You like food, but it doesn't show," I say. And we both laugh.

The others are concerned about food too. Fortuna had her kitchen paraphernalia but didn't have kerosene for her stove. Kenny had a small camping gas but needed to refill.

We all head for the village. I have no idea where what can be gotten, and market is not every day, so we have to troop around asking questions. I feel silly most of the time.

Sure, the villagers come out of their huts and stare at us. I see Bisi lounged against the trunk of a big tree, reading her New Practical English textbook. A small smile touches my lips, but I hide it. I remember my butt, and what her friends did.

She looks up from her book when we walk by. "Good afternoon, Tisha."

"Good afternoon," I mutter and move on with the rest.

After an hour or so, we have all the things we need for a good dinner. All at ridiculous prices but for now, we don't have a choice. I know the market opens twice a week so we can stock up.

Fortuna offers to cook for all of us. I buy three loaves of bread and restock my groceries since there are two of us now. I believe Jang will take the cue next time. Much of my finance comes from my mother, though the department pays a stipend. The school is expected to pay too but after six weeks and nothing, I doubt Mr. Akande will get around to it.

The evening moves fast. Fortuna cooks rice and vegetable stew. It is a sumptuous meal. Far better than Toro's. Or maybe I'm spoiling for a fight. She's still nowhere in sight but I'm not moved. She's a big girl and should take care of herself.

We retire to our rooms after a few hours of chatting and getting to know more about ourselves. The bed is too small for Jang and me, so I throw my blanket on the floor.

There's a knock on the door.

I answer without thinking. "Come in."

Kenny opens the door. "I thought as much."

I sit up. Jang seems to be asleep. "Hope no problem."

"Steve has still not come back and his number is not going. I thought Jang should come and sleep with me since the room is so big."

Jang sits up. "That's a good idea. I was feeling really bad for taking Abbey's bed."

"It's okay."

"It's not," Kenny says.

Jang takes his blanket and leaves with Kenny. "Goodnight."

I pull myself on to the bed. Grateful. With my body pains, I've wondered if sleeping on the floor will hurt me more. I can't sleep though. I'm getting a little worried about Toro. Where could she have gone? My initial thoughts of her being with Mr. Lagos seem far-fetched. He's a stranger. Would she trust someone she just met like that?

It's late now. Close to midnight. I stand. I have to look for her and probably send a text message to Mr. Akande. Toro has been gone for nearly twelve hours. It is strange. She may be a silly girl by my assessment, but even silly girls deserve someone to watch their backs.

I'm done dressing when I hear muffled laughter. I walk to the wall by Toro's room and listen. The wall is so thin I can hear her clearly.

"I'm not going to take that from you next time." Toro giggles. "Stop. It's late." Another deeper giggle. "Steve stop it. We'll wake everyone up."

"Let them wake."

I freeze. They start kissing noisily. He's up to something and she's a fool to let him do this. Today is the first day for goodness' sake! Was Toro this desperate?

"Steve, hmm."

I walk to my bed and lower myself on it.

"Oh yes, Steve. Steve."

She's a noisy lover. I hear every moan, and groan. I hear the zips of their clothing. I hear his deep grunts of satisfaction. I deduce he's a dirty lover.

Then she begins to scream with every thrust.

There's peace and quiet after another hour or so. My eyes remain wide open till close to dawn.

CHAPTER 11

BACK TO THE
STREAM

Horny and disoriented from a fevered sleep, I get up early and head for the stream.

Fortuna is brushing her teeth right in front of her room. Just what I hate. I'm not a tidy person, but litter and dirt drive me crazy. The rains have ceased and the harmattan sets in. The grass lawn in front of the block of rooms is drying up. If she doesn't pour water over the patch, it will look really irritating in a few hours. I reckon I will have to do it.

I shouldn't go to the stream till I leave Abagboro, but I miss the quiet and calm I experience upstream during those days we didn't have water, before the three boys flogged me with pronged whips.

It's just the breaking of the day and as I approach, I hear the villagers, mostly women, but the side I use is normally deserted.

I take the small path hardly noticeable and reach my place without detection. I feel a sense of peace and accomplishment. I dip my head in the water and come up dripping and wet. The water flows to the top of my shirt.

I'm helpless in controlling my thoughts. Reminders of the sexual act between Toro and Steve Eko, a man she just met, leaves me shaken. Jealousy I don't understand twist my innermost parts. I assure myself the jealousy is of brotherly love but I doubt.

I remain crouched at the edge of the stream till my calves give way then I pat the ground and make sure there are no stones but only wet dry leaves before I sit gingerly. Then I lay on my back to take some of the pressure off my wounds.

I close my eyes. The water on my head and face become chilly but it's just what I need. I'm not too much into women but I've had one or two and know what it's like. I don't miss it, and I don't want it… My heart beats faster. I go still. Maybe I do. Maybe I want it too much.

There's movement around me. Another assault? No.

I sit up just in time. Bisi. What's she doing here? She doesn't see me but walks to the other side of the stream just a few meters away, her back is turned to me. She calls to someone and tells the person to stay where they are. If I make noise, she will see me. She will startle, turn. I hold my breath. A hanging tree shields me a little, but I see her clearly.

She bends and removes her clothes from a wrapper. I'm confused now. Enthralled though. She has the same effect on me. Her movements are fluid, and graceful.

I quietly rest back and watch her. She washes the clothes she's brought with her, and chat with the other person on the other side. Does she know I come here? Besides those boys who found and assaulted me, no one ever came to this place. It is hidden and the water is cleaner.

I suspect this girl. It can't be a coincidence.

She finishes her washing and begins to undress. My head tells me to show my presence but the master between my legs object. I'm so turned on now, I can't believe it. Still my eyes are glued to her.

I am a carnal man, what is the devil trying to do to me? When I got my posting letter to Abagboro, I vowed I will keep my head. I didn't think I would face this kind of temptations but then just to be sure I know what I'm doing. I am only twenty-one. My anatomy longs for the natural things.

I can only see Bisi's backside but it's enough. Her skin is fair, and smooth and well-rounded. And I can't take my eyes off. She lathers herself languorously and hums a popularly church chorus.

I feel like the devil reincarnate. She must have come here for privacy and now I spy on her. I feel shame. Suddenly, the weather is hot, and no longer early morning coolness. I think I must have a full dip in the stream after she's gone or I will die here.

She finishes her bath and begins to rub cream on her body.

I die.

CHAPTER 12

CONFRONTATION

I do my Saturday washing on Sunday night because that's when I revive from death.

Toro and Steve hang around each other and play like little kids. Jang simply stays back in Kenny's room. So, I get to *enjoy* the noisy vocals alone at night.

The antibiotics I take have helped a lot and by Monday morning, I feel itching and sweet pain on the wounds. Sweet pain I wish someone could 'scratch' for me. Ahh, being a self-constrained bachelor does have its cons.

I have the first two periods on Monday in Bisi's class. After much energy getting certain images out of my brain, I get to work.

"Open your book to page fifty. Read."

"Today, Shinese food is well known around the world, and recipes for Shinese cooking can be found in most cookbooks and on many web sites. While books with some information about ancient Shinese food have survived the centuries, fascinating new information has come more recently from tombs."

I stare at her. "You've been practising. That's good."

She smiles. "Thank you, sir."

I swallow hard. Does she know what she does to me? "We have to work on your pronunciation of ch."

"Yes sir."

I look around and it seem we are alone. Everywhere is quiet. "Take your seat, thank you." I write summary on the board. "This is the same thing your seniors are doing. So, you should be proud. Can anyone else try to read?"

A few hands go up. Progress. There was a time last month no one in this class could read.

"Good. But you don't have to read it again. Now summary is a short sentence that represents the main points."

Teaching is my passion. I try to focus on my work but once every while I turn to the class and I see her, rubbing cream on her backside. The image is vivid.

I went back on Sunday morning. Call me carnal. This time I planned to reveal myself, let her know I come here too but she didn't show up. I need to confront her about it. I need to confront Toro as well, talk about respect for my privacy.

"Bisi, see me in the staff room before you go home," I say before I leave the class.

I have the whole day to plan my conversation with her. I need to confess to her I saw her and I need to know if she knew I was there. Fine, she'd come from another direction. My eyes had been closed when she arrived so she might have seen me and turned, depends on where she approached from. Also, shrubs are overgrown in that area and the branches of the trees serve as cover in some parts.

Toro walks to my table and perches on it just before the closing bell. "Why are you avoiding me, Abbey?"

I snicker. "You make a hell of a lot of noise when you're—happy."

She laughs. "Omg. You hear?"

"I dare not admit that."

She pats my cheek. "Poor Abbey. You are jealous."

I roll my eyes. Toro's too cheap. Cheap beauty. I spot Bisi loitering at the entrance. I need to know what her values are. Did she notice I was lounged on the grass by the stream and still continue with her bath?

"I hope he appreciates what you give him."

Toro smiles. "We'll see where it goes."

She seems genuinely happy and for the life of me, I do hope she's happy. Men like Steve and women like her roam till they find true love, as amazing as that sounds.

I nod toward the door. "I want to see a student."

Toro turns and sees Bisi. "Is that your distraction, Tisha *oko*?"

I'm amused at Toro's reference of me as a bush teacher. Isn't she one as well? "You like to look for trouble."

Toro doesn't move from my table. "Confess."

"No. Now will you excuse me? She's my best student so I want to ask her some questions." Toro still doesn't move. "Toro, will you move. Before your hot flame thinks I'm his competition."

"Hmm, you think that will work?" She arches her eyebrows. "Well, it did. We're going to Ife for lunch and shopping."

I sigh. "Have fun."

"We will." She winks at me and clicks her tongue at Bisi. Such a petty woman.

I wave to the seat in front of my table. "Bisi, sit down."

Bisi sits and folds her hands in her lap. My eyes follow her every gesture. There are a couple of teachers in the room both facing their businesses. I lower my voice all the same.

"So when are you going to learn to pronounce ch?" What am I talking about?

Her lips tremble. "I try sir."

CHAPTER 13

SATURDAY
RITUAL

An inner demonic clock wakes me on Saturday morning. It's a bit cold, and I put on my sweater. It is not logical, but I wear my canvas shoes and put on a face cap.

The walk to the stream is quick, like someone is on my trail. I shut out the voices in my head and pull the face cap closer. I shove my hands in my pocket and reach my upstream area when it's still dark. The stream is quiet. This way, I can't miss anyone's approach.

I pull out my handset from my pocket and use its light to survey the area. I notice a track that leads to where Bisi stood last Saturday. I follow it a little and realize it's quite close to the village. If she'd come that way, she'd have stopped before getting to where I lay and if she's not observant or never imagined anyone there, she'd not have seen me.

I feel a little relief and hang my benefits of doubt on that. I'm relieved she's not a loose girl who would take her bath on purpose knowing full well a man watched.

I find my way back to the spot I sat last week. It's mean and dirty of me to wait and hope. At least, I've made a logical discovery about her virtues. Instead, I lower myself to the same spot as last week and draw my face cap closer to my nose. It's now proven beyond doubt I am a shameless man, but no one needs to know that.

It's not yet 5a.m and I don't know how long I'll have to wait before she shows up, if she does. But I'm a patient man and considering the torture I've been through in the past few days, an hour or less is not a bad wait.

Some girls arrive the downside of the stream first, and make a lot of noise, swimming, jumping in and out of the shallower part. I lay on my back and wait, my heart beating so hard, I fear it will give me away. I don't even know if this is her Saturday ritual. I only hope.

I feel dirty, and stupid. And horny.

I hear her voice before I see her. "Stay there. I'm coming," she says in her dialect.

I ease myself to a sitting position and see her. Glorious evil, she's facing me now. I bite my lips. She can so easily see me. And she seems closer. It also means I will see her front view, and with darkness lifting...I break out in sweat.

She turns away and unties a big scarf of clothes. She makes small talk with the person she came with and starts to wash. It's boring to watch her wash but I endure. She will have her bath afterward.

My wait is not long. She packs the washed clothes into another scarf she earlier folded on the ground and begins to undress. She's a sight to watch. My heart beats rapidly. I swallow to ease my dry throat. She's so beautiful. I can't find the words to describe her.

It's worse, and better that she stands sideways almost to my full glare. I can see her bosom and oh my, clothes don't flatter her half as much as her natural endowments.

She rubs the local cheap 'soda' soap on her body, and soon, she's covered in white foam.

Then my 'china' phone rings.

In the dead quiet of the environment, it is an alarm.

Bisi turns toward my direction and screams. "Thief, thief!"

The person she was conversing with raises his voice, a male voice. "Where?"

She comes to bath with a man? Anger mingles with the fear clutched in my stomach. But right now, I need to escape. If I run through where I came from, it will be easy to see me and to know it's me or one of the youth corpers. It will be easy to investigate. It will be too humiliating. Instead I tear into the bush and run.

Bisi continues to scream and I can hear her loudly. The man she is with runs after me. The thick brush makes getting away difficult and to my dismay, I have to clear the path for the person behind me. Adrenaline pushes me on though, and I continue to run like my life depends on it.

My phone stops ringing and then starts again. How could I have forgotten to put it in silent knowing I planned to stalk Bisi while she's having a bath?

The man behind me throws a stone. It's small but it catches the tip of my ear. The pain is excruciating but I cannot stop now. I don't know where this bush leads to, or how close my assailant is. I lose breath but I keep running.

Another stone hits the back of my head and this time I trip and fall. I turn quickly and see no one. I crawl on my back and make to rise. But a third stone hits me between my eyes. The stoner shows up then, running. He's not even a man but I can swear the voice I heard was deep and cracked.

He's almost as fair as Bisi, and they have the same face. I know him from the school, Bisi's younger brother, Ajao, in junior secondary year two. I have to admit the boy is a good target. He looks as shocked to see me as I am to see him.

He holds a bag of stones hung around his neck, a hunter indeed. I slouch on my elbows. What a shame!

His deep voice is low now. "Tisha."

"Please, please don't tell Bisi."

CHAPTER 14

CLASSIFIED

I remain on my back long after Ajao left, a deep longing for a rewind seated in my belly.

Can I trust him to keep the secret? At least he turned and left without a word, which was as good as it was bad. He wasn't as bright as his sister, and I search within of any time I may have picked on him or his friends, whoever they were. Does Ajao have a bone to pick with me? And does he have his chance now?

My heart breaks at the disappointment I heard in his voice when he called me. Sure now, this may have happened before. It may be the reason why Bisi chose that secluded area to wash and bathe. It may be the reason why she brings her brother along each time.

I'd come every day since that last week, and now I can say at least she comes on Saturdays alone. But would she ever come again? What would Ajao tell her? If she knows it's me, how would she react?

My offensive phone rings again. I pick it this time. It's Toro.

"Aha, where are you? I've been calling since."

I need a word stronger than hate. "What's the problem?"

"Aren't you coming with us to Erin Ijesa again?"

"Erin Ijesa?"

"We planned to leave early for the waterfalls, remember? Where are you anyway?"

"I—at the stream. Go without me."

She sounds breathless. "Of course not. Only you will remain here? All the corpers are going even some students from OAU."

"I don't—"

"What did you go and do at the stream anyway? We're waiting for you, o!"

She hangs up.

Maybe I need sometime out to catch some fun. Since I arrived this village, I haven't gone anywhere. I've not even visited the famous Obafemi Awolowo University, Ife. I'd heard so much about OAU and yet I've been here for nearly two months without a visit. This is the opportunity. It will help me get out of my grouch as well.

I get to my feet and dust my trousers. And look around. I have no idea where I am or how to get out. I follow the direction I imagine I ran from, and the bush just thickens. I turn and follow another direction.

At some point, I imagine I hear the stream, and then voices but I can't trace it. Toro calls again but I refuse to pick her call. No use.

I roam around the bush for over an hour before I burst out to the village square. My heart thuds with frustration. How more stupid could I get? Thank God I'm not lost. To crown my shame, the group is in a small bus at the square. They stop when they see me.

God, why wasn't I missing for another hour or two?

"I've not had a bath. Go on without me."

"We'll wait for you," Toro says.

Steve scowls. "We've been waiting for him forever. Is he a baby? Please let's go!"

I nod. "Good word."

"What's your problem, Steve? You've been grouchy all morning."

"Can't you see the time? You're never conscious of time. You think everything and everybody will always wait for you and what you want?"

Toro rolls her eyes. "You don't have to shout."

To my shock, and I notice Jang gasp too, Steve pushes Toro's head. "Don't you ever roll your eyes at me?"

I throw my hands up in the air, not ready for any form of combat. "Okay. Please give me ten minutes, and I'll be back."

I run off despite my earlier fatigue running, and then roaming. Steve pushing Toro's head like that is just nonsense. That's what a girl gets when she hops in bed with a man the first day they meet.

CHAPTER 15

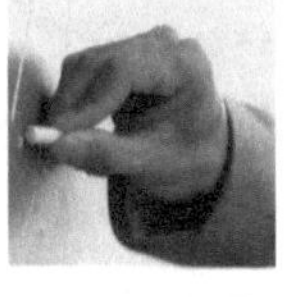

AJAO

I attend the church on Sunday morning as I normally do and sit at the back because I got there late.

The fun at the Erin Ijesa was just what I needed to lift off some of my burdens. Steve and Toro quarrel throughout the fun trip and for the first night in a week, I sleep without the x-rated vocals. Though I suspect I heard some in the early morning.

When it was just Toro and me, we attended the local Pentecostal assembly together but with a new lover who cares nothing about God or decorum, Toro has stayed back.

The pastor mercifully preached about something else, and not sin. I enjoy the service, but guilt embedded inside force me to go in search of Ajao.

In the spirit of reconciliation, I buy a loaf of bread and some biscuits, and a bottle of coke. This should appease the hot-headed stoner.

Most of the huts in the village are made of mud. A few are plastered with cement, and painted, like Mr. Akande's house. Bisi's house however has old mud bricks and thatched roof almost falling off and they live in the inter part of the village where the poorer people live. Bisi is under a huge guava tree, bent over her math textbook.

For a moment, I just study her while she's oblivious of my presence. Her long dark hair falls over her bent face.

I lose my voice for a second. How she affects me. "Bisi?"

She jumps up. "Tisha. Good afternoon, sir."

"Good afternoon. Did you go to church?"

"Yes sir. We go to Catholic."

"Okay." I look around. How do I ask for Ajao? What's the point of reference? I don't know any other members of her family. Wish I did.

I shove my hands in my pocket. She stares at me, wondering what I want, I guess.

"Can I sit?"

This girl will kill me with her beautiful eyes. Her lips part, and I have to look away.

She scoots and gives me space on the ground. I smile at her, appalled at how sweaty my palms feel, and dry my throat is, and heavy my heart beats.

"You live alone?" I chuckle. "With your parents, I mean."

"Yes sir. Ah, no, sir."

Good. She's nervous too. Of course I doubt it's for my reason. "Okay, yes you have a brother."

"Ajao. And my sister, Bimpe, and my other sister, Titilola."

"Ajao is your only brother?"

"No. I have big brother in Ife. He's mechanic. Dauda."

"Okay. So where are your other siblings? I see only you and Ajao in school."

"Bimpe and Titilola small. They are primary school."

"They're *in* primary school." I smile at her. I'm in love with her. No doubt about that. She nods. I know she won't make the mistake again. She's so hungry for knowledge.

A loud female call from behind the hut. "Bisi!"

"Ma!" She stands. "My mother. Calling me."

"Okay. Greet her for me."

"Yes sir." She runs into the hut.

I pick up her math textbook and look at it. Since Kenny came, he's taken over teaching the senior classes, so Toro now teaches the junior ones alone.

Bisi's notebook is very neat. The lessons Toro marked are full of corrections, but I notice a change from Kenny's teaching and marking. Bisi has improved.

My silly mind tells me there's rivalry between Toro and Bisi. So silly. I sigh and rest my back against the tree for a while. If only things were different. If only she was Toro, or someone else, not my student. I'll be drooling after her all over the place. The thought brings a lazy smile to my lips. Ah Abbey Ilori, in love with a village girl. A proper Lagos city boy. I still can't believe it.

I remember what brought me, and I stand up. If Ajao sees me here, he will feel angry. I would too.

I walk back to the road, looking left and right. I have no idea where Ajao is. But I don't want to leave the bag of peace offering I brought for him with Bisi. That will be suspicious. I am tempted to give the bag to Bisi but on what basis. I can't have an affair with her. I dare not, much as my body yearns for it.

I decide to pass by the stream, maybe I'll see Ajao. Two boys run into me, and the nylon bag tears, and the bread falls.

"Don't you look where you're going?" I curse. "Useless boys."

"Ah, Tisha. Is you?"

I look at the face of the one who spoke. It's the speaker of the three who assaulted me. I swallow and move forward quickly. He laughs at me and his friend joins in. I will find out who he is. I want to find Ajao first, and now more than before. If the boy is my friend, we kill two birds with a stone. He'll keep my secret and help identify this insolent boy. I know he's not in any of my English classes so he's probably not in school but he's an indigene of this village.

Close to the stream, I hear a sound of the water in a funny way and walk over to check. Ajao stands a little off the banks and throws stones into the stream, his small bag of stones hung around his neck.

I walk over. He turns at my approach.

"Tisha, hope nothing again o."

It is a war cry in my ears. I put on my best charm. Time to win a soul.

CHAPTER 16

BACKSTORY

I **stopped going to the stream early on Saturday to respect my friendship with Ajao.**

I discovered the boy was quite enterprising and his stone-sling brings home birds and small animals for food. We soon establish a teacher-student relationship where he taught me to sling and I teach him English.

A routine formed and many evenings during the week, we would meet at the stream. I wanted to learn to swim too. And he cheekily told me Bisi would have to teach me because she was a better swimmer.

I laugh. "She will run from me if I ask her."

"Tisha, she will." His eyes twinkle with mischief. "But if I ask her…"

"Don't ask."

He chuckles. "She will break my head."

It is early evening and we have finished both lessons for the day. I managed to strike a big wild bird for the first time, and we sit out at the edge of the forest and roast it together.

I laugh. "She will?"

"She's not quiet the way you see her in class. She's a troublesome girl."

I'm glad to hear about Bisi. Just the mention of her name thrills me. "Ah, troublesome, how?"

"Hmm, she can fight. If you look for her trouble."

I turn the bird on the spit, eager to know more. "Everybody's like that. If you look for my trouble too, I will give you."

"Tisha, no o. You are gentle. See the way—" He looks away. "You are gentle."

"See the way what?"

"They must never know I told you." He looks nervously around. "Or Bisi will be in trouble."

I swallow. I won't allow her to be in any kind of danger. "No one will know."

He focuses on the bird for a while. "My mother will be so happy when I give her this bird. She will make vegetable soup from it."

I follow his decision to change the subject. "You know, when I saw your mother, I was—shocked."

Ajao laughs. "Strangers are like that when they see her."

"She's almost white." I shrug. "How come? Though I know some foreigners come and do research and decide to stay back and live in the village." I shake my head. "But your mother speaks the dialect. Without even a small accent." I throw some dry sticks into the fire. "And I know I shouldn't talk like this with you, but I'm amazed she married your father."

Ajao grins. "Let me tell you the truth, Tisha. My mother is not a foreigner. In fact, her mother lives with us in the hut, but she is old and sick."

"And her father?"

"Nobody knows him or where he is or where he is from."

Amazing. I stare at Ajao. That must be tough for the family. From the way their mother looked, she definitely was half-caucasian. The few times I saw the beautiful woman who bore my love, she tied a scarf, but her skin is near-white. Bisi's hair is long and curly, and even Ajao's cut to the scalp has the telling curls of a mixed-race child.

"Our family is almost a taboo. People avoid us. Even after my father married my mother, people started hating him too. His family." Ajao narrows his eyes. "Grandma said she came home from the farm one day and realize she was pregnant. Two foreigners met her in the farm and forced their way with her." He removed the roasted bird. "I am so tempted to finish it here and now, Tisha." He smiles and my heart breaks.

"How old are you, Ajao?"

"Fourteen. Your Bisi is seventeen."

He stands and kicks dust into the makeshift fire. My Bisi. It sounded good in my ears but not what I should encourage him to say.

"You can't talk like that, Ajao."

"Ah, Tisha. I am only joking." He looks at me. "Will you follow me home so you can cut your half of the bird after I show my mother or—"

"Of course not. The whole bird is yours. It is such a small bird, how will we share?"

"Ah, Tisha. The bribe is enough o. I told you your secret is safe with me."

I control my temper. After all, he has kept the secret so far. "It is not a bribe. Give your mother. I don't cook in my house."

"You are so generous, Tisha. If not that we are so poor, I will revenge that stupid Ade who arranged for boys to beat you."

I freeze. "Is that what you said no one must hear or Bisi will be in trouble?"

He nods. "Tisha, the wind has ears. Let's go."

CHAPTER 17

SUITOR

Ajao insists I follow him home with the roast bird, sure his mother would want to appreciate me.

I find nothing wrong in that and silently pray Bisi will be in front of the house. Seeing her in school has gradually become not enough. I am approaching a fevered pitch, and each day seem more difficult than the last.

It's been a month since I was flogged at the stream and nothing has been heard from the state department concerning Toro's application. I'm not sure she wants to leave now, anyway.

Bisi is not in front of her hut, and my stomach sinks with disappointment. Lately, I dream of her waking up beside me. I see my hands comb through her curly locks. I see us in the stream, swimming naked.

"Good evening, Maami."

Ajao's voice tears me out of my mind-roam. He rises from where he prostrated to greet his mother.

I bend slightly as is the culture. "Good evening, Ma."

Bisi's mother's accent is worse than her daughter's. "Tisha, welcome o. Ajao, you brought Tisha to our house?"

"He killed this big hawk, Maami. And we roasted it together. And he now said I should take all of it."

"Ah, Tisha." The older woman goes on her knees.

I rush to catch her. "Ma, please. This is nothing. I don't cook so it will just get bad."

"You don't cook? Then Bisi can come and help you to cook."

I swallow at the prospect. "Ah no ma. Bisi should face her studies."

"Ah, Tisha. This is too much." She looks at Ajao. "Let me see the bird."

Ajao unwraps the old newspaper with the bird inside. "See Maami. It's a big bird."

"Ah Tisha! Ah thank you, God bless you." She laughs. "Take it inside." She turns toward the entrance of the hut. "Bisi! Bring the bunch of bananas I cut at the back this morning."

Ajao runs inside with the roasted bird.

I know the banana is for me, and I long to see Bisi. Still. "Let me take my leave, ma."

"Ah Tisha, wait please." She stands from the low bench from where she'd been shelling melon seeds. "Bisi!"

She has a considerable backside, which I notice Bisi is already developing. Someone once said you should look at your girl-friend's mother to know how your girl will look at that age. It doesn't always work, but in this case, I think it will. I hope it will.

Bisi comes out with a bunch of ripe bananas.

Her mother sighs. "Aha, take it and follow Tisha."

"Ma, thank you very much. Bisi doesn't have to follow me."

"No, let her carry it behind you."

Has the older woman sensed my heart's greatest desire? I bow, thank her again, and get on the way. Eager to be alone with Bisi.

She walks behind, which makes it impossible to converse. I don't want to be forward but really, I think I will have to let her know my feelings. It will scare the daylight out of her. Or maybe not.

When we get to the border of the school premises, I slow down. I don't want her near my room. The others would not understand especially after Toro's few insinuating comments to me about her.

"I think you should go back from here, thank you," I shove my hands in my pocket.

"Okay sir." She hesitates because I make no move to collect the bananas from her.

"I think your spoken English has improved." I smile. "Though you've still not mastered 'ch' I wonder why?"

Bisi shrugs and looks down.

My hand moves without my permission and I tilt her chin up. "Don't be shy with me, Bisi."

Her beautiful eyes widen. Her skin is as soft under my touch as I imagined it to be. I rub my thumb over her jaw despite the warning alarm in my brain. I could lose all six months of practical work if the department finds out I am in a relationship with any of my students, but this moment is too good to pass up.

It is semi-dark, and quiet, and anyone who would recognize us would have to come close.

"I will teach you, Bisi." My thumb touches her lower lip. "I can teach you many things." I continue to stroke her. "I'm sorry I beat you that day."

My voice is hitched in my throat. O God, help me walk away from here.

"I have to go back, sir," she says with a small voice.

It is louder than the early morning alarm in my ears. I take an uncertain step back. "You should." But I still don't take the bananas from her. I'm angry I have to leave her. Angry she has to be my student at this time, untouchable, unreachable.

She holds out the bananas to me. "Take sir."

I take the bananas and to my shock, Bisi turns and runs. I feel ashamed. I can only imagine the extent of the fear I read in her eyes when I caressed her chin. What must she be thinking?

I turn and walk slowly to my room. I imagine I will spend a long time under a cold shower tonight.

CHAPTER 18

ALUTA
QUARTERS

Gradually, everything settles around me.

The youth corpers catch their fun by going to Ife or the palm-wine joint in Abagboro, which I found amusing, because I never knew it existed. When I'm in the mood to have a refreshing, relaxing evening, I follow them. Much of my entertainment is to watch the village drunks display while the owner of the joint, a fat, dark-skinned woman called Iya Elemu I'd never met before, top up their cups.

"How does she get her money back?" I ask Kenny one of the evenings, when the woman kept refilling a man's cup despite the fact that he was dead drunk.

Kenny laughs. "Iya Elemu. She knows where she catches them o."

We return to our accommodation the corpers now tagged "Aluta Quarters" in a sober mood. Kenny is drunk and touching Fortuna indecently. She's tipsy as well. Jang did not follow us, never does because he is more committed to God than any of us.

Toro and Steve as usual are not in, or perhaps asleep or fighting. Hard to tell the things they do sometimes.

I prepare my bed and crawl in, glad to have this privacy to myself. I open my diary and write a poem for Bisi. It's my aphrodisiac. I'd written quite a few before, when I wanted her so much, a cold shower didn't do the trick.

In moments of want
I think of you
So far so near
I think of you
Through thin through thick
I think of you
I think of you
Though you don't know
I think of you
Though time will tell
I think of you
My love my life
Cos thoughts of you
Do feed my dream

I close my diary and hug it to me.

I hear Kenny and Fortuna talk a little too loud for the time of day. Jang paces the back of our windows praying aloud too.

I hug my diary to me and close my eyes.

The following evening, Foyeke comes to Aluta Quarters after school hours with a bowl of corn pap and local mixed vegetable soup.

Fortuna calls me over to Kenny's room for a meal. I never pass up an invitation to eat because I still don't cook. I'm surprised these teachers allow a student to cook for them. Even Jang, who seems usually disconnected from the rest of us joins in.

I feel a little uncomfortable with Foyeke and the cold rift between us but I ignore it for the sake of the others. The vegetable soup is well-cooked and tastes nice.

Kenny feeds the cold corn pap to Foyeke, and she feeds him too. My mind reels. I hope this is not a set up. Does Kenny know she's the village head's daughter? I don't want to associate with this. Yet, a quick glance around and I seem to be the only man uncomfortable, so I keep my thoughts to myself.

Steve and Toro arrive and come into the room.

"Just to say hi all, and we're back," Toro says at the doorway.

"I was smelling the soup about a mile away." Steve sits on the floor where we all surrounded the bowls of food. "My hands are clean." He dips his hand in the pap and touches it on the vegetable soup. "Hmmm."

"Aha, Steve. You're such a funny person. Don't you plan to eat the rice I boiled?"

"With your tasteless stew." He laughs. "Come and join us. This is very nice." Steve tweaks Foyeke's cheek and the silly girl laughs.

Kenny slaps Steve's hand and both men laugh. I look at Toro. She stares at Steve with a hard expression.

"Well, goodnight everyone."

"Goodnight, Toro."

I was the only who responded. We finish the meal and stand. Foyeke packs the bowls and takes them to the kitchenette. How many times has she done this? It is just not right.

"Thanks for the meal." I say to no one in particular. "Goodnight."

There's a chorus response. I leave the room, but the others remain. I'm not willing to get entangled in a student-teacher-student affair and I wish Steve would treat Toro with some more respect, regardless.

I'm morose and though I pull off my clothes and prepare for bed, I wonder if it is in my place to caution Toro. She's not a kid anyway, but I don't think she can take care of herself.

I curl on my bed and write a grieving poem for Bisi, then I hug the diary to my chest and close my eyes. Toro's side of the block is quiet, but the other side gets noisy. I suspect they are playing a game or so. I've seen them play cards several times, but I never joined in.

After a while, Fortuna opens her door next to mine on the other side. She hums for a while and I doze. But I am startled awake by consistent knocking.

"Abbey, are you awake? Please open up."

I jump to my feet. "Jang?"

"Yes. I want to sleep in your room."

I unlock the door. "What happened?"

Jang looks confused and disoriented. "I don't support this." He walks in and paces.

I lock the door and turn to him. "What?"

"She, the girl from the village, is spending the night."

I shrug. "I guess Kenny knows what he's doing." I sincerely hope.

Jang clenches his teeth. "And Steve?"

CHAPTER 19

RETALIATION

I hear the scream from two classes away, and the first time, I ignore it.

But I know that scream. Since she gave it to me, I've not been able to get it out of my mind. A swift tearing sound, and the scream again.

I look at the students I just gave a small classwork to do and walk to the entrance of the class. If I—the scream. I follow the sound and its Bisi's class like I guessed. And Bisi is doubled over, much the same way she did for me that horrible day not so long ago, her two hands squeezed in between her thighs.

Toro flogs all over her body while she waits for Bisi to present her hand. I swallow hard. If I intervene, would it not put Bisi in more trouble? What was Toro doing in the class, anyway, she no longer taught it.

Bisi straightens and stretches out her hand. From outside the window where I stand, I see the red welts on her already blistered hand. I look at Toro, and her face is stony. She raises the cane and hits hard on Bisi's hand. The poor girl screeches and falls to her knees.

I can't take it. Toro hits her on the head with the cane. "Stand up. Stupid girl."

I turn around and walk to the staff room.

I'm shaking so badly, I can't concentrate. It's true I cannot control who gets offended by her, but at the same time, I'm wondering what her offense is. Why would Toro be so cruel?

Shortly after, Toro walks into the staff room. She ignores me though I stare her down, bidding her to look my way. It doesn't happen. Again, I reconsider what the repercussion of challenging her would be. Was this a form of retaliation for hitting Steve? How petty.

She's been angry with me since the confrontation the day before, but I'm not bothered. One day, she will realize I did it for her.

I don't have Bisi's class today and thankfully too. I won't be able to teach seeing her in pain. I barely get through the rest of the day. I ignore Toro since she acts like nothing unusual has happened.

Later in the early evening, I go in search of Ajao. We have our evening lessons and hunting together. Maybe it's my mood, I catch nothing though Ajao got a small bird. We pluck the feathers and roast before I raise the topic.

"How's Bisi?"

He shrugs. "She's fine."

"And her hand?"

He arches his eyebrow. "How did you know?"

"I was teaching close by. I heard her."

Ajao shakes his head. "That female tisha is very wicked."

Anger rises from my stomach. "But what did Bisi do?"

"Nothing o." Ajao shakes his head. "She just enter the class, call her out, tell her she's very stupid and flogs her six strokes."

"I have to take that up with Toro." I take a deep breath. I know Toro will be glad she got at me, but that is so unfair and not justified. If she has any problem with me, she should face me, not a helpless girl who has nothing to do with it.

"How's the hand?"

"Swollen. But my grandmother has put some herbs so she can be able to write. The tisha just beat only her right hand. Six! Ah very wicked."

I swallow. I don't want to hear more. "What sort of herbs?"

"Local herbs. Very good one o. Then they wrap it with leaves and tie it."

"You know what, when we finish here, we will go to the drug store together and buy some drugs for her."

Ajao chuckles.

I frown. "What's funny?"

"You really like Bisi o."

I'm tempted to laugh but remember I can't afford to share such jokes with him.

I wag my finger. "You can't talk like that."

"I know." He laughs, and I hide my face to conceal my amusement.

We walk to the chemist together and I buy the drugs and bandage recommended by the shop owner.

"You should come and give her yourself, Tisha."

"No." I remember what happened last time. "You give her. Goodnight, and greet your parents."

I rush off. My blood is hot, and I want Toro to explain some things to me. I hope she will be available.

She is not. But not for the reason I expected.

I find Toro locked in combat with Fortuna. They tear at their hairs and underwear. I am appalled not only by the sight of the two ladies fighting shamelessly in front of the block, but Steve and Kenny playing *Ludo* inside Kenny's room, with the door ajar.

I fling my backpack to one side and throw myself in between the girls.

I gasp. "What is wrong with you both?"

They ignore me and reach around me, so I carry Toro who is the smaller of the two to her room. Fortuna follows, and I barricade her.

"Fortuna, stop it."

Fortuna pants. "Let me teach the little fool a lesson of her life."

"You are a big fool, Fortuna." Toro yells from inside her room. "*Asewo*! Husband snatcher. *Ole*! Thief!"

Fortuna pushes at me but I hold her at bay. "Abbey, get out of my way."

I lower my voice. "Look at you, you're bleeding. What's this about?"

She turns and walks into her room. I follow her. Steve's sharp laughter cuts through the night sounds. I need to speak with these guys later on. This is so not acceptable.

Fortuna looks into a small mirror to view the damage caused by Toro's sharp nails on her cheekbone. The cut is deep and ugly.

"What happened?" I say softly.

Fortuna is such a simple and agreeable girl, I never could have imagined.

"Abbey, it's okay it's over." She picks a small towel and cleans around the wound.

"You'll need antiseptics for that. I have some in my room."

I rush to get my small first aid box. "Here." I put some antiseptic liquid on a cotton bud. "It will hurt a little."

She stifles a scream and grabs my hand but lets me clean her.

I look at her pointedly. "You need to sleep. Take two Panadol tablets and just try and sleep."

"She's such an idiot, Abbey." Fortuna bites her lips. "She thinks everyone is sleeping with Steve."

I can't believe my ears. They fight over that? Toro's insults make sense to me.

"Did you?" I don't know why I ask. "I'm sorry I asked. It's none of my business."

"Yes." She smirks. "And I will do it again just to spite her."

I rest my case. No wonder the guys play while the girls fight.

CHAPTER 20

PASSION

Jang moved out to live with our village Pentecostal church pastor, and I can't blame him.

If I had a choice, I would move too. Nothing more has been heard of Toro's report and request to be transferred based on my assault experience. I suspect Mr. Akande must have swept things under the carpet because it wasn't good for his reputation or that of the school.

Life goes on. The hostility between Toro and Fortuna hurts deeper than I expected. After all, we're all strangers here and may never cross paths again after we leave. Steve shows no remorse. I heard him in Toro's room later in the night, and they made 'animal' love. It leaves me totally sickened at the nauseating behaviour of these so-called adults.

They all went out the following evening. Toro and the guys to Iya Elemu, and Fortuna to Ife to visit her friend on campus.

Home alone, I pick up an old favourite from Richard North Patterson, Eyes of a Child. I've read it twice already, and each time seem like a new read.

I'm hardly through the first chapter when there's a knock on my door.

"Who's it?"

There's no response, only a knock again. I wear my trousers and put on a shirt.

"Who is it?"

No response. I open the door anyway, and there at my door, is Bisi. I do a double take and look around. It's dusk and getting cold on this late November evening.

My heart thuds. What does she want? Alone, and here. I thank God the others are out. And then pray against that. I don't trust myself alone with her.

"Good evening, sir." She curtsies. "My mother said I bring food for you."

"Food?" I step back. "Come in."

"Yes, sir."

I close the door behind us. I'm finding it hard to control my breathing with her so close. There's nothing unique about her shabby clothing but her lips look soft, and her plaited hair hang around her face. She puts the nylon bag in her hand on my small table and turn toward the door.

"What did your mother cook for me?"

She turns. "Pounded yam, and vegetable soup."

I shove my shaky hands in my pocket. "Why?"

"To tell you, thank you." She licks her lips. "For buying drug for me."

I lean against my wall. My legs begin to tremble too. "Ah, that's very nice of her. And she said you should bring it for me? Alone?"

She looks down, and shrugs.

"How's your hand?"

"Is better."

"Let me see it."

Her eyes shoot up to mine. I feel so hot for her now I can't think straight. She holds out her bandaged hand to me. I reach for it and pull her close. Part of her wrist is wrapped too and gently, I untie the wound, angry beyond reason.

No teacher has the right to do this to a student no matter what their offence. The hand is swollen and tender. Red welts slash across upraised, two open wounds. The pain she must have gone through. For a moment I consider taking pictures and do exactly what Toro did about my back, but then, I reconsider. What will come out of there in this outback?

My voice cracks. "What did you do to her to deserve this?"

"I—nothing."

I trace the wound on her hand. "She just entered the class and started beating you, she didn't say anything?" I look at her. "And she beat only you?"

She nods. "She said I am stupid. By the time she beat me finish, no tisha go look me again."

"No teacher will look at me again."

She nods.

I examine the wounds. It looks clean, which was what the chemist had insisted on. I wrap the hand back in the bandage.

"Was that all she said?"

"Yes."

"So, which teacher has been looking at you?"

She shrugs. I continue to hold her sick hand in both of mine. "You don't know, or you don't want to tell me."

She looks down. "I don't know."

I raise her chin with one hand. Her skin is just so soft. Her lips are pink and full, and so beautiful.

"Tell me," I whisper.

She licks her lip again and I want to capture her small pink tongue before it disappears inside her mouth. My palms are near freezing now, and my temperature risen.

"The new biology tisha."

"Steve." I swallow hard. "What did he do to you?"

"Tosh my hair."

At least she's not suffered because of my altercation with Steve. "The bas—" I bite hard on my teeth. "What else did he do?"

She looks down and I bring her face back up. I'm so furious I could break Steve's head with a bottle. What was the meaning of this?

"Nothing."

"Tell me the truth, Bisi. Did he touch you anywhere else? Did he kiss you?"

She frowns, and in my madness and lack of self-control, I bend and take her lips with mine.

I pull her fully into my embrace and enjoy what I have dreamed of for so long. It takes a while before I realize she's struggling against me.

I break off but place her head on my shoulder. "I'm sorry, I'm sorry." I twist her locks in my fingers. "I've loved you from the first day I saw you, darling."

I'm finished. How could I lose control like that? I lick my lips and capture her after-taste. I bury my head in her shoulder. Her body is full, luscious. She smells of local condiments and stew, and mixed with her female scents, I'm totally consumed by lust.

"If Steve ever comes near you again, tell me." I don't know what I will do. I pull back and look into her eyes. "Did he kiss you?"

She nods and looks away. My heart crushes into a million pieces.

"What else did he do?" I smooth back her hair from her face. "Please tell me."

"Nothing."

I feel as bad as Steve, but I am genuine, and I don't play around. "Are you sure, Bisi?" She nods. "Bisi, if he calls you again, call me. I mean that. Don't ever let him touch you again."

She nods. I'm ashamed I allowed myself to be carried away. "I'm not like Steve. Do you believe that?"

She nods. I stare at her. I want to tell her I love her but hold back. I've said and done more than enough already.

"I have to go back," she says.

"I will walk with you."

I tuck in my shirt and find a novel from my wardrobe. I'd always wanted to give her a book to read because it will help her English. I have a nice collection of books used for literature and I pick So Long A Letter.

I give her the book and encourage her to read it, then I walk her close to her house, and turn back home, unable to say anything about what happened in my room tonight.

Embarrassed. Mortified.

CHAPTER 21

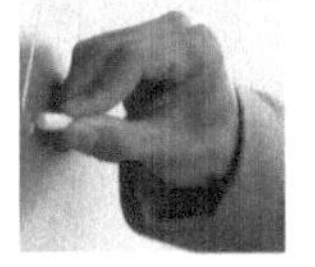

FIRE FIRE

I **can't eat when I get back.**

I want Bisi. I want her to understand me. I am not like Steve. How could he? Touch her, kiss her! I pace around like a defeated demon. I don't know what to do with Steve. There's no authority to report him to. This outback in the middle of nowhere is despised. Anyone can do anything and before the protocols in the state departments are observed, the culprits have moved on.

Only jungle justice works in places like this. I think of Ajao. Can he arrange for some boys to beat Steve up, just like what happened to me? For the first time, I really think of the boy Ade, Foyeke's brother. I'd learnt the boy was just a year older than Foyeke and dropped out of school three years earlier to be 'Prince of Abagboro.' If he could get boys to hurt me like that, he can do it again, for a price, I guess.

I've never arranged a hit on anyone before but definitely, this is well-deserved. Steve has come to mess around with everybody and he has to be stopped. Now I know four girls he's toying with and Bisi being one of them drives me crazy.

Ade took out revenge on me because I beat up his sister. He can do the same for me if I tell him Steve is now sleeping with his sister and cheating on her. There's a way to paint the picture that should set him off. Doing threesomes with Kenny, sharing a room with Toro and cheating on Toro with Fortuna.

I wonder if these ladies have any scruples at all themselves. How do girls just allow gigolos like Steve to enter between their legs? Left for Toro, she's using Steve as much as he's using her, but she's deceived.

I drop my head in my hands and sit on the edge of my bed. No matter who or why, all I want is for Steve to leave Bisi alone. He could have a million girls for all I cared.

My mind roams to the kiss I shared with Bisi. It was just as wonderful as I dreamed it, though she didn't respond.

I chuckle. "How sweet she will be when she learns to respond to me."

Thoughts of having a proper relationship with her propel me back to the food she brought. I'd better eat. Not likely my neighbours will return soon or be in the mood to share their food with me. I'd planned to eat my normal meal of bread and coke but what a sumptuous provision. The soup tasted better than anything I'd eaten before.

The pounded yam is more than I can finish, and I wish Jang was here. The slender man could eat a mountain.

I finish my food, what I can eat of it, and pack the rest away, hoping it will not be bad in the morning, and I can eat it again. Then I pick up my diary.

Words fail me to capture the few minutes Bisi spent in my room. I need to record my emotions, my joy and elation, my pain and disappointment, the heated passion I never knew was imbedded in me, and lust so overwhelming it is love.

I fall asleep clutching my diary and pen to my chest. Bisi, I love you.

Loud banging on my door wakes me. I jump off the bed and reach for the door in two leaps. I don't even ask who.

"Ajao!"

Ajao pants in front of my door. I look around and seeing no one, pull him inside.

He bends over and breathes hard. "Tisha. Tisha."

I check my watch on the table. It's after midnight. "What's the matter? Is it Bisi? Or your mother." I shake him. "Ajao! Talk!"

"Pastor said I should call you." He sits on the floor. "The other Tisha Jang. Say I should call you now now."

"What happened?"

"Ade, Ade *ti pa* Tisha ooo!"

Ti pa. I know *pa* means kill. I shake him real hard.

"Ade killed who?"

"The female tisha that beat Bisi. Ade has killed her ooo!"

"Yee! Toro."

I slip my feet into my slippers, grab my phone and rush out of the room with him. Fire on the mountain, run, run, run.

CHAPTER 22

MADNESS

There's commotion everywhere.

The pastor of the Pentecostal church has a rickety car, and at Iya Elemu's joint the car is parked with all the doors open.

I rush to the car, hoping Toro is already inside, hoping she's not dead. But Toro is not inside the car. Steve is, covered in blood. The whole village is awake and at the joint. I push people aside looking for the pastor, looking for Toro, looking for Jang, or Kenny. Anyone to explain what is going on.

Bisi is seated on the floor, still clothed the way she came to my house. What is she doing here? Her legs her wide apart and she wails like one in mourning. I notice blotches of blood on her body.

I see Jang finally and rush to him.

"Jang, wha—"

"Not now, Abbey." He paces, praying in tongues fervently. "Pastor has gone to look for petrol. The one in his car cannot take the victims to Ife. Hopefully, Baba Elero will have some—"

"Victims." I grab Jang. "What happened?"

His lips tremble like he will cry. "I called Fortuna. She promises to come with a cab. But it's late. I don't know."

"What happened here, Jang? Where's Toro, and Kenny? I see Steve in Pastor's car."

"Kenny escaped." Jang sighs. "The boy Ajao came to call Pastor."

"You've not said what happened. Who did this?"

"They were drinking. Six boys with machetes came here. They went for Toro. Steve tried to protect her." Jang pulls himself away from me. "I need to pray, Abbey. Call Fortuna and find out where she is."

Just then a car drives into the area raising dust at top speed. People scatter to avoid being hit. Fortuna jumps out of the car before it stops and run to us.

She screams. "Where are they?"

"Inside the hut." Jang heads inside. Fortuna and I follow.

Toro is in a pool of blood on the floor. I fall on my knees beside her but a man who ran in after us pushes me aside.

"I'm a doctor. Don't lift her," the man shouts.

Another man comes inside and carefully, they examine Toro.

"She's alive but losing too much blood." The man looks at his colleague. "Call the hospital. We need O+ blood on standby. God help us if she's a negative."

They carefully lift her to the car. She looks lifeless and I can only pray they can save her. Six boys with machetes! This Ade needs to be stopped. I can't believe he came for Toro, and why would it matter to him if she beat Bisi or not. No one touched his sister this time.

I feel some respect for Steve for the first time, and sincerely pray he doesn't die. The car Fortuna came with takes both victims away, and we have to wait for Pastor to return so we can go with him to the teaching hospital.

There's blood everywhere. Iya Elemu and her serving girls are nowhere in sight. Jang holds and pats Fortuna who is an emotional wreck. I walk to where Bisi is a bit calm and squat beside her. I need some real answers here.

"Bisi."

She hiccups. I rub her back, and she quiets.

"What happened? Were you here?"

She nods is her characteristic way and shifts from me. I feel deflated. Now she can't stand my touch. I look around and notice people are around. Of course, it is foolish of me to touch her in public. She's obvious of the people around. I sit beside her but not close and keep my hands to myself.

"Tell me everything that happened. Why did you come here after I took you home? Is this the kind of place you should be?"

She glares at me and her eyes tear again. I get impatient, and anger rises within me. Does she think her tears will move me from getting the truth out of her? Why would she come to such a place like this? And all the blood on her dress shows she must have gotten involved.

"I was sleeping. Ade come call me. Say where is Tisha Toro?"

Ade. The prince. Why would he go to Bisi's house? The truth begins to dawn on me even before Bisi says it. I wasn't punished for flogging Foyeke his sister. I was given twelve strokes of a wire-whip for giving Bisi one stroke of the cane.

I give Bisi a stroke and receive twelve. Toro gives her six and gets attacked by six machete boys. What an animal Ade is?

"Yes?"

"I beg him to leave her alone. Say my hand is okay." Bisi sniffs. "He pull me said we will go your house and I will call Tisha Toro to follow us."

"You know what he did to me because I beat you the other time?"

She nods. "I beg him to leave you alone. He no hear me."

I close my eyes for a moment. "Does he know what Steve did with you?"

"Heh, he will kill Tisha Steve."

Explains it all. That's if he hasn't already killed *Tisha* Steve. And if Bisi gets angry with me, I'm dead meat. The mad dog Ade is in love with Bisi too. What a reveal.

Bisi lowers her voice. "He was with his friends. He said me and him will watch his friends rape Tisha Toro, then they will beat her with cutlass. Six six all of them."

I shudder at the plan. Ade needed to be arrested. The boy was mad. No other explanation for this.

"He did not want to kill her ooo." She begins to wail again.

I look around. Many villagers have left. "So, what happened?"

"I tell him Tisha Toro has gone to Ife with you. He no believe. So he drag me to your house. I knock on Tisha Toro door, and everywhere is quiet. Ade now say he knows they drink and we came come came here."

I stare at her, angry, and sorry at the same time. I will let her finish before I ask my question.

"Then what happened?"

She draws in a deep breathe. "They were all drinking. We arrive, all of us. As people see us arrive, they carry their bottle and leave. Ade call Tisha Toro to follow us. She no gree. Tisha Steve stand up and face them." She sobs. "They cut him and grab Tisha Toro. I was crying and begging. Everybody run."

My throat clogs. "Did they follow the plan?"

Bisi looks at me, tears run down her eyes, and nose. And she nods.

CHAPTER 23

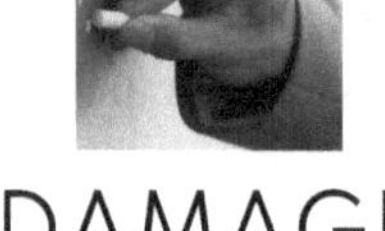

DAMAGE

Beyond words and expression, I just stare out into the surrounding darkness.

Bisi continues to sob and I find nowhere in my heart to console her. Five men rape a twenty-year-old girl and force a seventeen year old to watch. Nothing can be more brutal. There is no law. No order. I cannot ask where Ade is at this moment. Probably snoring on his wretched mat.

Pastor returns with only a gallon of petrol but enthuses that it will take us to Ife. We all get into his car, and despite my protests, Bisi insists she will follow us.

It's close to 2a.m. and my headaches now pounds in my eyes as well. One evil image remains embedded in my brain – Toro with those six evil boys. If I feel so bad, I wonder how Bisi must feel.

The petrol in Pastor's jalopy old Datsun car takes us to the gate of Obafemi Awolowo University Teaching hospital, and rolls to a stop. We all run out and head for the Casualty and Emergency accident area.

Panting and disoriented, we are turned here and there before someone attends to us. Thankfully, Pastor seems to be known in the emergency ward. A nurse on duty calls him aside and gives him a brief.

Steve was B.I.D.

"What's B.I.D.?" I swallow. "Pastor, I don't understand."

Pastor shakes his head. "Brought in dead, Abbey."

A cold wave of nausea overpowers me, and I stagger back for a moment. What a waste. Poor Steve. To think I was so upset with him just a few hours earlier and plotting to have him punished by the animal who killed him. I feel shame flood over me.

Fortuna screams and faints. Jang grabs her before she hits the floor, but her weight is a little too much for him, and he hits the floor on one knee. He lowers her to the ground and looks up, tears stream down his face.

"I tried to win him. Oh God!" Jang wept.

"Only one strike of the machete," Pastor whispered. "The killer hit him across his head to his neck. It was a deadly blow. He couldn't have survived."

I hear Bisi sob beside me. She shouldn't have come along. I am in no position to comfort her, much as I wished.

Steve was a huge guy. The killer must have been big too, and highly skilled. Just a blow had terminated his life. Oh death, where is your victory.

"What about Toro?"

I cannot forget my friend. How she came to be here beats my imagination. Maybe I should have taken her hints and had an affair with her. All these chain reactions would not have occurred.

Pastor takes a deep breath. "She's in the theatre. The doctors are battling for her life."

Fortuna stirs and proceeds on a loud wail that makes the nurse on duty to send us out of the waiting area.

It's cold and I notice Bisi's Ankara dress is short-sleeved. I pull my jacket, which I'd taken at a last minute, but change my mind. A wild beast is jealous over her at this moment. I don't want to be a subject to his bitter rage.

We spend the next two hours just lamenting the evil over Abagboro by this useless act. We all ignore Bisi who seem to have an endless capacity to shed tears. Her eyes are bloodshot and swollen almost shut yet, the tears continue to stream down her cheeks.

I wonder what kind of affection the evil Ade must have for her. Did she feel the same for him? I have a strange feeling he's not a potential suitor like me. But this is not the time nor the place to find out.

The nurse who'd supply the information comes out to us at about 5a.m.

"She'll live."

We all shout. Fortuna falls on her knees. I cover my mouth to keep from screaming. Thank God.

The nurse pulls Pastor aside and mumble a few things. Pastor nods once and returns to us.

"Bro. Abbey, we need to contact her family. She's been attended to only because of the doctors who brought her in," Pastor says. "Now they need money."

I bring out my phone. "I will call her sister. She used my phone to call once and saved the number."

"Be discreet. Don't get anyone excited."

I nod and walk aside to make the call. I didn't have to say more than was needful. Toro's sister goes ballistics on the phone. Finally, someone calms her and thanks me for calling, with a promise to come right away. Toro came from Ondo, a city about an hour away so I expect her family to arrive shortly.

About half an hour later, Mr. Akande arrives with the acting vice principal and Biology teacher, Mr. Ojo.

I am relieved to see them. Though of what use they are, I don't know. Pastor breaks the news and Mr. Akande, for the first time since I took up work under him, breaks down.

He points at Bisi amidst tears. "You! You again?"

I steal a glance at Bisi, and her lips begin to tremble again. Seriously, there can't be any tears left in her system. I am worried by Mr. Akande's accusation. "This happened before?"

"Yes," Mr. Akande sobs. "Oh God, what will happen now? Youth Service! They will never send anyone to Abagboro again. How will we cope?"

Mr. Ojo taps him, and hands him a phone. "The zonal coordinator of the NYSC is on the line, sir."

CHAPTER 24

NO CONTROL

CHAPTER 24 – NO CONTROL

After the traumatic call to the zonal coordinator of the NYSC, Mr. Akande and Mr. Ojo sat on the ground and waited with us.

I move to where the principal sat. I need to hear this. Has Bisi been here before? Why was nothing ever done? The love of my life, I am more concerned for her safety now.

"Sir, you said this happened before—"

The old man must have been waiting to pour it out. "Three years ago, a boy's body was found at the bank of the stream. He had suffered a deadly machete blow on the head." I gasp but allow him to continue. "I can never forget him. His name was Babatunde Ajala. His parents were poor farmers. Had lands with Bisi's family. Quiet people. They only wanted the best for their children." He sighs. "For months no one knew what happened to him. The police station charged with Abagboro is at least thirty minutes trek away. When they finally came to investigate, the boy had been buried by his parents. Counted their loss and moved on."

"How did it concern Bisi?"

Mr. Ojo turns to us. "Bisi was interrogated because she had been at the stream with Babatunde Ajala. It was rumoured they were lovers."

I gasp. "She was only fourteen." A quick glance at Bisi and I notice she has tucked her head between her laps but her shoulders shudder like she was in tears.

"As you can see, she's the most beautiful girl in the village. All the boys want her." Mr. Akande hisses. "But she had a special likeness to Babatunde. He was eighteen, in his final year in the high school. A great potential. Quiet, smart, handsome boy."

I feel a twinge of jealousy, which is quickly squashed.

Mr. Ojo sighs. "I think they both knew the danger in being lovers because they were very discreet. They met at the stream at odd hours in odd places."

Maybe they met in that awkward corner Bisi liked to bathe, I think.

"Well, one of Babatunde's friends knew about the affair and in the moment of pain and anger, blurted that Bisi knew Babatunde's killer." Mr. Akande sniffs. "We took her to my office and described to us what happened."

When Mr. Akande did not say anything further and Mr. Ojo too kept quiet, I yielded to the urge to prompt them, but Jang beat me to it.

He frowned. "What happened?"

"Bisi and Babatunde were at the stream alone. Ade came with two of his friends. One had a whip, the other had a machete. They asked Babatunde to follow them, he refused. Bisi promised the wild boys he will never see Babatunde again if they just go." Mr. Akande opens his mouth to continue but nothing comes out.

Mr. Ojo takes it up. "The boy with the machete strikes Babatunde. They carry Bisi and leave."

Fortuna whispers. "Where did they take her to?"

Mr. Akande shrugs. "She said they took her home. They did not hurt her. But Ade warned her she was his. Anyone he catches with her will follow Babatunde's footsteps."

No wonder she is so reserved. I look at her just less than a meter away from us, seated on the ground, her hands wound over her head. What pain she must feel, knowing Babatunde died because of her.

Jang raises his voice. "And what was done to the Ade?"

Mr. Akande sighs. "What could be done? He was Babatunde's classmate at the time. We expelled him from the school. But the police didn't do anything. Said they didn't have any evidence against him except for what Bisi said. And Bisi wasn't willing to make a written statement at the police—"

Bisi's head shoots up. "He said he will burn my father's farm." She sobs.

"What an animal," I mutter.

Pastor shakes his head. "He calls her the princess. Gives gifts to her family. He paid a dowry too."

I gasp. "A dowry!"

"Yes." Pastor snickers. "The only reason she doesn't live with him is because she's still in school. Her father made that deal with Ade. Pleaded to let her finish school."

I look at Bisi. She's technically married if the dowry has been paid. A furious anger wells up in me. Was high school education enough? What next after? She'll be the wife of the village prince. When the village head dies, she will be the queen, married to the meanest a@#$%^ words cannot describe. She will be the most miserable of all women.

And my heart bleeds for her.

"But what is the Babatunde's family doing? I mean what did they do? Their son died for nothing?"

Fortuna's question irritates the intellectual in me. "What do you think they could have done? They are poor farmers."

Fortuna rasps. "So?"

"Ade is the richest boy in the village. Even his father is terrified by him. Lets him get away with anything," Pastor says softly.

"Exactly. He's the prince. He has money, he has influence." I hate to say it. "And he has the prettiest girl."

Fortuna hisses. "Rotten riches."

"More than anyone else." I shut my eyes.

I want to believe this is a nightmare. I should wake up in my bed, my diary clutched in my hand. I should laugh at how feverish I am because of a kiss with Bisi. But this is a reality.

Everyone has walked on eggshells around Bisi because of Ade. He has turned her into a shadow of herself by the evil he has committed because of her. Much of her timidity now makes sense to me.

How come no one warned us? As visitors in the village, no one ever gave a hint. Bisi kept to herself most of the time, and out of trouble. The only friend I ever saw her with was Foyeke, Ade's sister. Maybe she assumed Ade would not hurt his own sister and so believes it is safer to be friends with her.

But an animal will always be an animal. What was it like being betrothed to such a mean person? I can't imagine but yet still, I see. Bisi is not a happy girl.

Everywhere is quiet again. I imagine we will be here till the hospital's administrative staff report to work and reports made, and the NYSC coordinator arrives, and Toro's family too.

It is such a long day ahead.

CHAPTER 25

AN EYE FOR A LIFE

It takes so little a time to drift from life to death, consciousness to unconsciousness.

I doze, and startle awake to some commotion. I look around and see everyone is alert as well.

Kenny jumps down from the bucket of a police van, wild and sweating copiously. Up till then, I had totally forgotten about him. Ah, here he is with police. Thank God someone at least is willing to book the criminals.

His clothes is torn, and dirty, and he is barefooted. Pastor meets up with him.

"I went to the police and took them back to Abagboro but everyone said they were brought here." His lips tremble. "How are they?"

"Toro is out of the worst situation for now," Pastor says. "We lost Steve."

Kenny's head drops to his chest. When he looks up, his eyes are awash, but they connect with Bisi's.

"What is she doing here?" Kenny yells. "This is the girl who brought them! Why is she here?"

I glance at Bisi, and she's on her feet. I'm confused again. She seems petrified. How was she the one who brought them? Had she lied to me? But if she was one of them, why would she insist on following us? Maybe guilt. Maybe she wanted Toro punished but not killed.

Kenny is on the verge of hysteria. He grabs the policemen with him. "Arrest her. She's one of them."

I jump in front of Bisi. What am I doing? "No, she's not, Kenny. You are mistaken."

"I know what I am talking about, I was there, you were not." Kenny gripped the shirt of one of the policemen and pushed him to me. "Arrest her."

"Calm down, Brother Kenny," Pastor says. "What happened? Thank God you were there."

Kenny heaves. "We were drinking. Toro was getting a little tipsy and wanted to leave. These boys walk into the compound. Immediately, some people carry their bottles and leave. Iya Elemu ask the boys to sit. Told them they could have drinks on the house."

Kenny points at Bisi. "Then this girl step forward and says they didn't come for drinks. She was wearing this same dress." Kenny sucks in his breath. "She asked Toro to follow them." He can't hold it anymore, and sobs. "We suspected it can't be for good. The girl said, Tisha Toro you flogged me. Today, you will pay. An eye for a life."

My mouth drops open. I turn to Bisi, and she just stares. "That's not true." I blurt.

"Tell her to deny it!" Kenny cries. "Steve stood up. He was drunk. He told them to get out." Kenny sobs hard. "One of the boys. He's not even so much taller than me. He strikes Steve and Steve drops.

Everybody ran at that time. I ran too. I was so far gone, close to the school before I remembered Toro.

"I ran back but she was gone. They were all gone. I didn't know what to do. I ran to the police station at the next village, but they didn't have staff and vehicle. I started coming here."

I pity Kenny. I pity all of us.

Pastor frowns. "To Ife?"

Kenny nods. "It's only here I could get policemen and a vehicle. When we got back to Abagboro, I was told what happened, and that we should come here. To the hospital." He turns to me. "Abbey, let them take the girl."

"Is it true, Bisi? Is that what happened?"

The girl I fell for looks different for a moment. Her eyes are still blood-shot and puffy, but the quiet way she looks through me sends shudders through my bones. Have I mistaken something? She's no longer crying and seems removed from everything around her.

Bisi meets me eye to eye. "Yes, it's true."

CHAPTER 26

DAMAGE CONTROL

I **stand back and watch Bisi's pliant hands put in hand-cuffs.**

I stand back and watch Bisi's pliant hands put in handcuffs.

I can't believe she admits it. Kenny's words are highly implicating. If this is true, she has a murder case, and an attempted murder to answer to. Murder in Nigeria is punishable by death.

Kenny insists there are witnesses who heard Bisi accuse Toro. And Toro is still alive. Hopefully she will make it out, and able to testify against the boys who did this to her.

I stand beside the police van just before it pulls away with Bisi. I need this moment with her. She remains on the floor of the bucket where she was pushed into, her eyes glued to a particular spot on her handcuffs.

"Bisi."

She doesn't look at me, much as I wish she would. It's only me and her. Kenny talks to the policemen and insist he'd rather stay back at the hospital and come later to the station.

I reach out and pat her roughened hair back. She flinches but doesn't look up. I may never understand but my feelings for her has not changed.

"I will come and look for you at the police station. Don't be afraid."

A small sob escapes her lips. Her hair is so soft under my touch and I don't care if anyone sees us at this time. She needs my support and I will give her. I wipe the tears in her eyes, something I've longed to do all night.

"Once we're finished here, I will come to the station. Hmm?"

She gives me her small characteristic nod and I step away from the van as it pulls away. I am right, and if I am wrong, so be it.

Mr. Akande walks up to me. "That girl is trouble, Abbey. If you want to leave this state alive, let her alone."

"But she—"

"She has survived without you till now. And she will survive after you're gone."

He walks away with that and stands by Mr. Ojo to await the expected arrivals.

First is Toro's sister and her husband. Once she steps out of a black Nissan Almera, I notice the resemblance. She runs into the emergency ward, ignoring us. Her husband hurries after her. Moments later they rush out and go to Mr. Ojo who points to Mr. Akande. I am still by the road where Bisi left me, and not inclined by any means to take part in this tedious task of answering their questions.

Nonetheless, I got a finger directed at me and Toro's sister and her husband walk over. They don't introduce themselves and bombard me with questions. I answer the ones I can. They join us in waiting and pacing.

Then comes the staff of the hospital and Toro's sister follows them to regularize the necessary paperwork.

The toughest part of the morning is when the officials of the National Youth Service Corp (NYSC) arrived. Mr. Akande is virtually wobbly on his feet. Six men and two women are in the team, escorted by two policemen, who interrogate us all. Kenny becomes a total mess when the zonal coordinator questions him.

At about 2p.m., I am finally free to leave.

The NYSC officials claimed Steve's body and signed for it. An ambulance arrived and took his body away. I assume they will send the body to his family in the South-South region of the country. What a colossal waste.

The doctors Fortuna called upon, who were known to the friend she visited on the campus, meet up with us.

"She's not conscious yet. She may not be for some time because her condition is not stable," one of them explains Toro's condition.

It's what we were told before so what's new? I bite my lower lip. "Will she be alright?" The doctor hesitates, and I add quickly. "I have an idea of what they did to her."

"Well, we suspect a disc in her spine may have ruptured. We can't do anything about it now, till she's more stable. Otherwise, she lost a lot of blood, and sustained other minor cuts." The doctor shrugs. "She will be fine. Let's just pray for her."

Ding dong not-merry bells ring in my brain. "Her spine. She may not walk again."

"It shouldn't get to that."

The two doctors walk away.

With Steve's body gone, and Toro's family here, I reckon I have other important matters to attend to. Bisi is in police custody. I shudder at what I imagine they could do to her.

Fortuna opts to return to her friend and later come to Abagboro, though the NYSC zonal coordinator issued a recall to the three of them immediately and gave them a vehicle to take them to the village to pack their belongings.

It meant I will sleep alone tonight.

I get a lift with Pastor who graciously offers to escort me first to the police station to find Bisi.

"With the youth corpers leaving today, you can move into my house, so you won't be alone in your quarters."

They were sweet words to a weary soul.

"Thank you, Pastor." I nod. "I'm most grateful."

CHAPTER 27

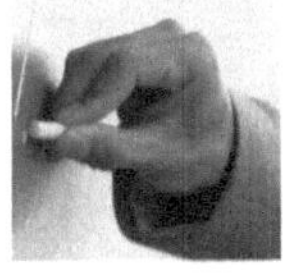

FIGHTING
TEMPTERS

If not for Pastor's presence, I would not see Bisi.

Despite that, we are moved from one location to the other until we are asked to wait. The wait ends up for two hours. I plead with Pastor to leave but he refuses. We've both not slept in almost twenty hours, but he doesn't complain. I am humbled by his genuineness.

When Bisi is led out to us, still in handcuffs, I am speechless by how badly she's been beaten. I thought they didn't maltreat female inmates. And she hasn't even been charged with anything?

She sits on the rickety bench offered us because her legs are so wobbly she can't stand without support.

"Pastor, how do we get her out of here, please," I say when I find my voice.

Pastor brings out his phone. "Wow, it's almost dead. But I will send a text message to an old school mate of mine who is now a lawyer in Ife here. He will meet us here."

"Thank you, sir."

He proceeds to send the text message. My phone's battery is dead, and I doubt any of the policemen here will let me charge. I pray his friend is in town and sees the message on time.

In the meanwhile, I study Bisi. She is calm. It's as if she's finally where she wants to be.

"Have you eaten?"

She shakes her head. "I am not hungry."

The mention of food reminds me I haven't eaten either. "You'll be alright." She nods.

Pastor looks at us. "I have sent the text message. I pray the battery lasts for him to respond." He pats Bisi's knee. "Just tell the truth. It will set you free."

We sit quiet till Pastor's friend arrives about an hour later. Pastor's integrity had allowed the policemen to leave Bisi with us.

The man Pastor simply refers to as Barrister is tall and slim, and dressed for court in white shirt and black trousers with his white collar still on.

He greets us both warmly. "The news is all over town. I was worried for you." Barrister looks at Pastor. "I hope you are okay?"

Pastor smiles. "God is faithful. I am fine."

Barrister shares his gaze between the three of us. "So how can I help you?"

I blurt. "We need her to be bailed. She's innocent."

"Well, we need to see the police report. It she's in for murder, it's a different ball game all together." Barrister sighs. "I will talk to the policemen in charge now and get a true picture."

Bisi moves closer to me and whispers, "Please can I tell you something, alone?"

I tap Pastor and repeat the request. The men stand.

"We'll go and see the arresting officer," Pastor says, and leaves with Barrister.

"Bisi."

"Tisha, leave me here. Let the police do me anything they want."

Her words hit me on the wrong side. "Of course not."

"Yes, Tisha. Let me die here."

"Bisi, don't talk like that. I will get you out of here."

She shakes her head. "Nobody fit find Ade. And Tisha Kenny is right. Na me tell Tisha Toro to come out."

I notice she speaks badly when she's nervous or scared. "Why did you do that? Why did you ask Toro to follow you? You knew what they were going to do to her."

"I know knew."

"So why did you tell her to follow."

She shrugs. "Well, I no want leave here. Make I suffer for my problem. Tell Pastor to take the Barrister away. You too, go. Sir."

"Bisi?"

She stands. "Yes. Sir."

"Come on, sit down. What's wrong with you?"

She smiles. The first time I will ever see her smile. And she looks so beautiful. I spot a dimple on one cheek and my heart fails me.

"Tisha Abbey, go home." She walks to the counter and the police officer behind opens it for her.

"Bisi! Bisi!"

What's wrong with her? She wants to die here? I walk to the officer and demand he brings her back.

The officer laughs. "Criminal wey kill two people? Leave all these village girls o, bros."

I rush out to find Pastor. They can't be charging her for murder until they investigate. This is what I fear most about the system. Kenny says she talked and now she's guilty of murder.

Bisi has to fight for herself. She can't give up like this. And they have to find the animal, Ade.

Pastor and Barrister are outside the premises of the station, talking easy.

"Pastor, we have to—"

"Ah, Bro. Abbey, we were just waiting for you to come out." Pastor frowns. "There's a new development. Good news mainly."

"Okay sir, thank God."

"Toro is awake and has been talking a little. She has said everything that happened."

I want to rejoice but the frown on Pastor's face confuses me. "Thank God."

"Bisi is guilty. She's the mastermind of everything. The police have refused her bail until there is a court hearing."

CHAPTER 28

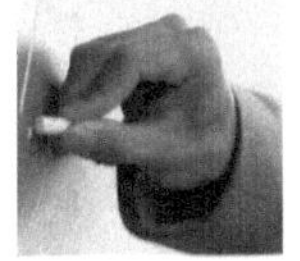

BISI

We arrive my block at a quarter after five.

My bones are weary, and I am drained of any motivation. The block I deserted, and I wonder at how much could have happened in such a short period of time. How life and death has changed everything.

Pastor magnanimously wait for me to pack my bags. I look at the food Bisi brought last night, now sour, and tears gather in my eyes.

"God, please help her. Help Bisi."

I throw the food away and wash the bowls. Then I tidy the room and rush back to Pastor.

Close to 6p.m I finally enter Pastor's house. It's my first time there. His wife, a frail-looking woman who serves in the prayer department of the church welcomes me. I am taken to the room Jang used, which I discover is being used by three other young men from the village, stewards in the church.

The parsonage is a small modern bungalow, painted blue inside but left plastered alone outside, and situated at the back of the church building.

I find Pastor seated outside the house with his wife. "I need to go and see Bisi's family, sir."

Pastor's wife looks at me. "Food is almost ready."

"I will eat when I return, ma. Thank you."

I walk to the hut at the backside of the village. Everywhere is quiet.

"Knock knock." I call out. "Who is in, please?"

Bisi's father steps out. I have seen him only a few times and from a distance. He looks in his fifties but today, like thirty years has been added. I respect him. From the tales Ajao told me, his father has fought many wars to marry his wife and keep his home.

"Tisha, welcome," he says in a low gruff voice.

I prostrate in the cultural manner. "Good evening, sir."

He pulls up a low bench and sits. "They say my daughter killed the two Tishas."

I sit beside him. "She did not, Papa."

"Ajao has gone to Ife. To the big brother. To look for her."

My heart bleeds. "She—"

"She is a precious baby. When I met her mother, they were living in the forest. Her grandmother gave birth to a white baby and was thrown out of the village." He sighs. "I fell in love with her the first time. She was just the way Bisi looks now. Even prettier."

Bisi's mother comes out with a bowl of water. "Good evening, Tisha."

I bow. "Good evening, ma. Thank you for the food you sent to me yesterday."

"My son, thank you." She mumbles something to her husband. He grunts.

She exits and returns with food, which she places in front of us. I protest but Bisi's father will have none of it.

"Eat, Tisha. Even if it is small. We are not rich, but we are good people."

I open the bowl. I should have brought the bowls they used the day before, but I forgot. The bowls contain the same soup of yesterday and a mound of *garri*. I cut a small morsel and eat slowly.

"I know you like Bisi. I see the way you look at her."

I nearly choke and take a quick sip of water from the cup in front of me. I feel shy to take any more food.

"I want her to have a good man. Like you." He nods. "I told you earlier that she's special. I had my first son and ten years later before Bisi came. And she opened the way for Ajao and the other girls."

"She's very special, sir," I say, for want of what else to say.

He sobs. "Ajao say they lock her up like a criminal."

His sudden outburst takes what little is left of my appetite. "I will get her out of there, sir."

"Please, please do."

He bends over and covers his head. I stand quietly, distraught. I walk out into the night. I don't know what to do with Bisi now. Pastor doesn't seem interested in getting involved. The barrister, I don't know. I can't leave her in police custody and there's no way to get her out without the services of a lawyer.

Many thoughts cross my mind, and the final one leads me to the last place a sane mind will advise.

The Abagboro clan head lives in the largest compound in the village. The main house, a bungalow surrounded by a thick mud wall fence is surrounded by three smaller bungalows where I'd presumed his wives and children lived. When we first arrived, Mr. Akande had taken Toro and I to visit the old man in his palace.

At the time, we had been expected and a guard had waited outside to take us in. Now, I'm alone and the surrounding is deserted.

I stand before a wooden gate painted green and contemplate if it's not rude to bang on it. I may enter the palace and end up in trouble. I don't want that. I walk around the mud hut but meet no one and my intuition advised I leave.

I feel broken inside out, helpless, frustrated. What can I do? My mind zigzags toward thoughts of the worst possible outcome. If Bisi never gets out of prison. But my resolve takes me back to what I must do even if it costs me my life.

I consider visiting Mr. Akande or Iya Elemu but doubt it will be of any use at this time. Maybe tomorrow morning I can convince Pastor to take me to Ade's father. Ade has to come out and own up to what he did.

I return to Pastor's residence at about midnight. I have not slept in close to twenty-four hours. When I lay on the bed, a few words run through my mind and I grab my diary.

Bisi

I see, you have taken me over

Bisi

I hear, you are a jewel and a prize

Bisi

I know, I will never find joy

Bisi

Unless I find it with you

Bisi

CHAPTER 29

ALAS

The following day, I wake up to prayers in the house and a splitting headache.

After the morning devotions, during which I expected prayers to be made for Bisi, but was not, I decide to get on this journey on my own. As long as I have a bed to sleep in Pastor's house, he has done enough for me.

I was offered breakfast, of which I took a slice of bread and a cup of tea out of mere politeness. I am a man on a mission and until I accomplish it, I will not rest. I dreamt of Bisi again, at the stream, taking a skinny dip with me. Though, it wasn't my face, it was the face of—Babatunde Ajala.

Why did I think it was the dead boy? Too much thinking.

First, I head for Ife. It's Thursday and I have classes, but I doubt anything will be in order in my life until my Bisi is out and free. The painful part is no one has even mentioned the boys with the machetes.

At least, if Bisi killed two people, she must have a machete in her hand. And if she ordered the hit, as they claim, then the killer should be apprehended too.

I am not allowed to see Toro because I am not family. I wait outside the ICU for an hour before I take another decision. I could check on Bisi too.

The decision doesn't pay off. The police don't allow me to see her. I do the unthinkable, a man on fire, and tip off one of the uniformed men. He leads me to a small, empty cell at the back of the station, and locks me in. My heart thuds. Have I made a mistake? Am I in trouble? Though if I am, the officer would not have locked me in with my mobile phone. I begin to send a text about my location and activities to my sister, but the officer shows up with Bisi.

I put my phone away and glare at her. She looks a little better than the day before. At least, there are no fresh bruises on her face. Her dress is torn at the shoulders and dirty, and she's barefooted. Still, she looks so pretty.

The policeman opens the cell and she walks in. He locks it behind her and turns his back on us but doesn't go away. I don't care if anyone watches. I pull Bisi into my arms and kiss her hungrily.

"Sorry," I murmur when the kiss is over. I smooth back her hair and place her head on my chest. "You'll be fine. I promise you."

Bisi's hands hang down beside her. I wish she will hug me back, but it's all in a matter of time. Maybe she's still in love with Babatunde Ajala. Maybe she's afraid to love me so Ade will not kill me too. Whatever her reason, I will give her time. As it is, I have broken the code of professional conduct by showing her any affection. I feel bad but helpless and encouraged that her father has given me consent anyhow.

Bisi grips my shirt front. "Tisha, don't come here again."

I lift her face to mine. "Why, darling?"

"I no want you to come here. Is not a good place."

"But you're here. If you are here, I want to come and see you." She shakes her head. I nod. "Yes. And all that talk about leaving you to die here, God forbid. I will do everything to get you out of here."

She stares me down and finally looks away.

"Bisi, do you know how we can find Ade? He has to come out and confess."

She snickers. "You can never find Ade."

"Why not? Did he leave the village?"

She shrugs. "He is there. He is in the village. He is in his house."

"At the palace?"

"Yes."

"So I can get police men to arrest him?"

"Tisha, he will kill you o." She pulls out of my embrace and hugs her arms around her waist. "Tisha, just go."

"I promised your father I will get you out."

I thought that will excite her, shock or encourage her. Instead she shrugs. "My father has no power. Ade will get me out when it is time."

Her words unscrew a bolt in my brain. "Ade will get you out?"

"He knows what to do."

My pulse races. "He knows what to do? And when will he do it? When is time for him to get you out?"

She leans her head against the iron bars of the cell. "Tisha, please go."

A sudden coldness hits the core of my innermost being. "Okay, I will go. Let Ade come and take you out. The same boy who gets you into trouble is the one you want, right?" I hit the bars. "Right?" She jumps and I curse my anger.

I pace the small space, thinking. How can she say that to me? How can she want this Ade animal instead of me?

"Fine." I throw my hands up. "Fine, go back and wait for Ade to bail you out." I grab the cell door and raise my voice. "Officer, we're done."

The policeman opens the cell and lets us out. He disappears with her and I find my way out of the station. She didn't even look at me. Not even a single backward glance.

My trip to Ife is in vain. I want to beat something. I find it difficult to focus. What next, what next? The realization that she wants an evil animal defeats me and I lose the inner energy to fight for her.

I return to the teaching hospital and thankfully, I find Toro's sister at the ICU. She smiles and welcomes me. At least someone appreciates my efforts. A spontaneous thought occurs to me and I give her my mobile phone.

"Since Toro is talking now, please can you tell her to tell you everything that happened on Tuesday night and record for me?"

CHAPTER 30

BID YOU WELL

Bisi may be in love with a beast but I love her, I know. It's wrong, and heaven knows I tried my best to control my feelings. If I am discovered, I could repeat a whole year because if the practice period is cancelled, I'd have to take the year again. I am ready to be penalized because I love her. On the other hand, with Steve's death and Toro's attack, I may be taken out of the village too, if my department hears about this, coupled with the previous assault on me.

I return to Abagboro earlier but don't feel inclined to go to school. It's just noon. School is in session, and the parsonage is deserted too. Probably Pastor is in the church office. I don't know what his wife does but the house is locked. I sit outside and contemplate. I need to listen to the recording of Toro's account of the events, but I don't want to be disturbed.

I take a walk to the stream, notorious now for all the evil stories. I find my imagination going wild, thinking of Bisi and Babatunde having an affair, kissing maybe or doing other things.

To make my life more miserable, I go over to the secluded area Bisi uses and sit on the ground.

Toro's voice is thin but clear. "Is Steve okay?"

The response comes from a stronger version of Toro's. I assume it's her sister. "Yes, dear."

"Why hasn't he come to visit me?"

"He's not family, dear. They won't let him into ICU."

"But he can come with you." She pauses. "They cut his head. Are you sure he's okay? Have you seen him?"

My heart beats fast.

"Yes, I've seen him. They stitched the cut so he's also in the hospital."

"But you said he's fine."

"He is, Toro dear. He is." Pause. "I need you to tell me everything that happened that night. So, the police can arrest the bad boys."

"But Steve knows."

"Yes. He has told us his part. After they took you away, what happened?"

I listen with stiff attention. My palms sweat and I shudder at how well Toro recants. Can she ever get over this? Poor girl. I wish I had pursued the application to be removed from this hell-dump, like Toro will put it.

I am sure our departments never investigated the village before sending us here otherwise they would have known about the murder of Babatunde Ajala and any other atrocities committed by Ade.

I tuck my phone into my pocket and stand. I am pushed down. I fall on my back and lift up on my elbow. I didn't hear anyone approach. I look up and stare into the deadly cold eyes of my worst enemy. Ade.

He is alone and I figure I can tackle him in combat. He is a little shorter than me and not much bigger. I dart my eyes around. He is alone. Good.

"They tell me you've been hanging around the princess," he says.

His voice is as cold as I remember. Colourless.

"I don't know what you're talking about."

He lights a crude roll and puffs several times. I recognize the smell of marijuana. Definitely a beast must have something to get high on. He will kill me too. The ugly thought runs through my mind. I remember my mother and sister. They will be devastated if I die.

"Bisi. Princess Bisi." He leans back on his heels. "You visited her. Kissed her."

A huge stone rises into my throat from my stomach. Death where is your sting? If I die, I die. From what I gathered, this evil, ugly thing is my age mate. Why should I be afraid of him?

"I want her out of police custody, and you are the only one able to do it. That's what she said."

He smiles. A flash of a tilt of his lips that doesn't near reach his eyes. He takes more puffs. "She knows her man."

A second person shows up beside him. The whip at my assault. I look at his hand and he has a machete in it.

The hitman's accent is thick. He looks at Ade. "Should I split him in half?"

I think fast. "Of what use will I be to you dead?"

Ade smirks. "None. You will be useless to my princess too. Alive. Or dead. Whatever."

"I will leave your village, if you want. But please get Bisi out of the cell."

He kicks my face and my head rolls into the sandy bank. "Ah, see your blood on my shoe, Tisha."

I taste blood. I turn my face up. Let him kill me staring me in the eye.

"Tisha, I will leave you for now. Not because you are of use to me, but my princess has an odd respect for you. And right now, she's confused and unhappy about all that happened recently. If you like yourself, stay away from us. Do your job and respect yourself. You won't even know I exist if you stay in your corner I stay in mine. That was how things were before you beat my princess. And your friends start to mess around."

His words swirl around my head. He continues to smoke and talk. I wonder how a man can have so much junk to say. My head feels heavy and I can't quite comprehend what he's saying. He rolls another joint and smokes it all.

On his third roll, he says, "I bid you well, Tisha." And leaves with his executioner.

I get back to the parsonage several hours later. News has it Bisi is back home. I fight the urge to visit her. Instead, I apply to Mr. Akande and the state department for my transfer.

Whether it is approved or not, I'm done here. I count my losses and move on with my life.

THE END.

Acknowledgments

I wish to thank all my followers on my blog www.sinmisolao.wordpress.com for the great feedback I got on TISHA while it was on the blog. I want to appreciate my husband, Afolarin Ogúnyinka for the support and information he helped to supply on the research for the book. I thank God for everything, and everything else.

The Nigerian Child: My Vision

Then the LORD answered me and said: "Write the vision and make it plain on tablets, that he may run who reads it." —Hab. 2:2

More than before, it's time for the well-to-do to cater for the less privileged. Over the past few years, the Lord has laid this burden for The Nigerian Child on my heart, and I believe it's time to spread the vision. I have a desire to help and to instigate help for The Nigerian Child. There are currently five areas of help I have been able to identify.

1.	The Market-school Project: This vision is aimed at eradicating street and market hawking in the long run. The strategy is to erect schools in marketplaces where children hawking can take a few hours out to learn and then go back to their jobs. It is a long-term project and a highly capital intensive one.

2.	The Bread and Milk Project: Bread and milk will be given in the morning to children trekking to school just before school resumes. It can be done once a month, once a week, or every day or as rampantly as the provision is available. It is not very capital intensive, and as little as N50 or $0.35 USD can feed a child with bread and warm milk.

3.   The Umbrella Project: This will help alleviate the suffering of children who hawk on the streets (while we work toward eradicating hawking on our streets) by providing umbrellas, especially during the rainy season. The umbrellas can also be useful during the scorching hot weathers. Umbrellas of different sizes will be given depending on the size of the child. Prices of umbrellas range from N350.00 to N500.00 or $2.50 to $3.50 USD.

4.   The Sort-a-child Project: This is aimed at helping at least a child in whatever capacity you can. It can be by paying a sick child's hospital bills, buying food and clothing for a child, or paying a child's school fees. It can be as long as a lifetime commitment or a onetime affair.

5.   The Student Care Project: This is for secondary and tertiary students who can't afford their school fees. The idea is to help through the bob-a-job initiative.

The Nigerian Child vision is not another nongovernmental, money-spinning organisation. It is service to God and provision for The Nigerian Child. It can be done privately or corporately. The important thing is to help a Nigerian child.

I beg to challenge every church in Nigeria to adopt the sort-a-child project or as the Lord lay it on our hearts.

HELP! Signed

- THE NIGERIAN CHILD

SCATTERED

NOVELS:
TO WHERE THE WIND BLEW (BOOK 1, EIBA FAMILY SAGA)
SCENT OF WATER
PEPPER
FRAIL FLESH
THE DAYS AFTER THAT NIGHT

WISDOM SERIES:
WISDOM FOR MEN
WISDOM FOR PASTORS
WISDOM FOR WOMEN
WISDOM FOR PASTORS' WIVES
WISDOM FOR SINGLES
WISDOM FOR NEWLYWEDS

ISSUES OF LIFE SERIES (CO-AUTHORED WITH AFOLARIN OGÚNYINKA):
SOMEBODY HELP! SHE LOVES MY HUSBAND
SOMEBODY HELP! HE LOVES MY WIFE
SOMEBODY HELP! I'M IN LOVE
NO IS NOT NEGATIVE
SOME GOD USE, SOME USE GOD

REVELATION SERIES:
CHOICE